BREAKOUT

GOLD HOCKEY #6

ELISE FABER

BREAKOUT
BY ELISE FABER
Newsletter sign-up

This is a work of fiction. Names, places, characters, and events are fictitious in every regard. Any similarities to actual events and persons, living or dead, are purely coincidental. Any trademarks, service marks, product names, or named features are assumed to be the property of their respective owners, and are used only for reference. There is no implied endorsement if any of these terms are used. Except for review purposes, the reproduction of this book in whole or part, electronically or mechanically, constitutes a copyright violation.

GOLD HOCKEY SERIES

Gold Cast of Characters

Heroes and Heroines:

Brit Plantain (Blocked) — first female goalie in the NHL, loves boy bands

Stefan Barie (Blocked) — captain of the Gold

Sara Jetty (Backhand) — artist and figure skater

Mike Stewart (Backhand) —defenseman for the Gold, romance guru

Blane Hart (Boarding) — center for the Gold, number 22

Mandy Shallows (Boarding) — trainer and physical therapist

Max Montgomery (Benched) — defensemen for the Gold, giant nerd

Angelica Shallows (Benched) — engineer at RoboTech, also a giant nerd

Blue Anderson (Breakaway) — top forward in the league and for the Gold

Anna Hayes (Breakaway) — Max's former nanny, no relation to Kevin Hayes

Rebecca Stravokraus (Breakout) — Gold publicist, makes killer brownies, known at PR-Rebecca

Kevin Hayes (Breakout) — forward for the Gold, no relation to Anna Hayes

Rebecca Hallbright (Checked) — nutritionist for the Gold, plethora of delicious vegan recipes, known as Nutrionist-Rebecca

Gabe Carter (Checked) — doctor, head trainer for the Gold

Calle Stevens (Coasting) — assistant coach for the Gold, former national team member

Coop Armstrong (Coasting) — talented forward on the Gold, addicted to historical romance audiobooks

Mia Caldwell (Centered) — 5th degree black belt, brings the snark

Liam Williamson (Centered) — Gold forward finding his love for the game, charming and pushy in equal measures

Charlotte Harris (Charging) — new Gold GM, hates losing and the game Chubby Bunny

Logan Walker (Charging) — defensemen for the Gold, skills include: cockiness and being able to buy presents that make Charlotte squirm

Devon Scott (Block & Tackle) — former player, current owner Prestige Media group

Becca Scott (Block & Tackle) — Devon's assistant

Additional Characters:

Bernard — head coach

Richie — equipment manager

Dan Plantain — Brit's brother

Diane Barie — Stefan's mom

Pierre Barie — Stefan's dad, owner of the Gold

Spence — former goalie, married to Monique, daughter Mirabel

Monique — married to Spence, former model

Mirabel — daughter of Spence and Monique

Mitch — Sara's boss

Allison and Sean — Blane's parents

Pascal — Devon Scott's security lead

Roger Shallows — Mandy's dad

Grant and Megan — Devon's parents

Because sometimes you'll find a person who's worth being inside your armor.
Don't be afraid to let them.

Prologue

PR-Rebecca

Now *that* was a fucking photo op.

Blue and Anna, young lovebirds, had their hands pressed together, only a layer of glass separating them, her big burly hockey player telling his fiancée he loved her.

The hockey blogs were going to eat this shit up.

"Instagram," she murmured, fingers flying across the screen of her iPad, cropping and trimming the video into a short and snappy GIF.

Blue would hate it.

But Rebecca didn't give a damn.

This was—no pun intended—solid Gold shit.

She slapped on a filter, one that emphasized the Gold's logo on Anna's beanie, then posted the video.

"Fucking. Perfect," she said, eyes glued to her screen as she began scrolling through the rest of the camera angles and making her way to the ice. Her DSLR hung around her neck, ready to capture any high quality stills the press might miss in their effort to document hockey, rather than what was really important, at least from her perspective.

The story.

What made people care.

What turned them into lifelong fans.

What went viral.

And Blue and Anna would go viral.

Maybe Brit and Stefan, too, helmets tossed to the ice, arms around one another as they kissed full on the lips.

And all of that at center ice, music blaring, lights flashing. It was—

"A fucking perfect hockey fairy tale."

Shaking her head, because she knew firsthand that fairy tales didn't exist outside of rom-coms and occasionally between alpha sports heroes and their chosen mates, Rebecca slipped through the corridor and stepped onto the Gold's bench.

Lots of dudes in suits—of both the boardroom *and* the hockey variety—were hugging.

On the ice. Near the goals. On the bench.

It was a proverbial hug-fest.

And she was the cynical bitch who couldn't enjoy the fact that the team she was with had just won the biggest hockey prize of them all.

"I knew you'd be like this."

Rebecca turned her focus from Brit, who was skating with the huge silver cup, to the man—no, to the *boy* because no matter how pretty and yummy he was, Kevin was still a decade younger than her—leaning oh so casually against the boards.

"Nice goal," she told him.

A shrug. "Blue made a nice pass."

And dammit, the fact that he wasn't an arrogant son of a bitch made her like him more.

She nodded at the cup. "You should go have your turn."

"I'll get mine," he said with another shrug.

She frowned, honestly confused. "You don't want—"

Suddenly he was in front of her on the bench, towering over

her even though she was wearing her four-inch power heels. "You know what I want?"

Rebecca couldn't speak. Her breath had whooshed out of her in the presence of all that sweaty, hockey god-ness. Fuck he was pretty and gorgeous and . . . so fucking masculine that her thighs actually clenched together.

She wanted to climb him like a stripper pole.

"Do you?" he asked again when her words wouldn't come. "Want to know what I want?"

She nodded.

He bent, lips to her ear. "You, babe," he whispered. "I. Want. You."

Then he straightened and jumped back onto the ice, leaving her gaping after him like she had less than two brain cells in her skull.

The worst part?

She wanted him, too.

Had wanted him since the moment she'd laid eyes on the sexy as sin hockey god.

"Trouble," she murmured. "I'm in *so* much fucking trouble."

ONE

PR-Rebecca

"Oh my God, this is the best thing ever," she moaned, letting her head drop back onto the table.

Off-season made for good perks.

"If you stopped wearing those torturous death traps, I wouldn't need to do this." Mandy pointed to Rebecca's heels, which her friend had stolen then tossed haphazardly on the floor, despite the fact that they cost more than her rent . . . and considering she lived in San Francisco, that was saying a whole hell of a lot. Her friend had commandeered her, probably because she was bored and with the season more than a month from getting underway, her training suite was sadly empty.

Hence the thieved heels and stern order for Rebecca to hop on top of the leather-covered table.

"Girl," Rebecca declared, moaning again when Mandy's firm fingers slid up to her calves. "If there's one thing I'm never going to turn down, it's a foot massage. They are the only surefire way into my panties."

"Ew." Her friend broke into peals of laughter. "But noted. Been a long time?"

Rebecca sighed and flopped an arm over her face. "Long enough for me to re-virginize."

Fingers dutifully digging into the tense muscles, Mandy said, "I know there's plenty of guys sniffing around."

"I'm not interested in men."

A pause, long enough for Rebecca to move her arm and glance up at Mandy. "What?"

"Is there something I missed?"

Rebecca rolled her eyes. "I'm straight—well, there was that one time in college, but that's not the point."

"Um."

"Everyone experiments."

"Um."

"And anyway, my point was that men are unreliable and pathetic and useless."

Mandy's fingers stilled. "Um."

"Stop with the *um*'s," Rebecca said. "It's true." Well, aside from Stefan and Blane and Mike and Blue and Max . . . Okay fine, so perhaps it was more about her shitty choice in men and less about the opposite sex. Not that she was going to admit that. Nope. No fucking way.

"Why'd you stop?" she said, less about the massage and more about stopping herself from blurting out a retraction—or maybe it would be an amendment?—to her previous statement.

Mandy smirked, hands moving again. "So, those are some strong feelings."

"Well, strong feelings come from strong personal experience," she muttered, then because she might spin stories as a career but couldn't peddle bullshit to her friends, added, "And I'm not saying *your* man is that way . . ."

A chuckle. "Just the rest of them?"

She grinned. "Exactly."

"How's the baby?"

Mandy's expression softened, gorgeous brown eyes turning to melted chocolate. "She's amazing." An adorable frown that competed with her little girl's cuteness. "And growing way too fast."

"Blane showed me that video you took of her the other day," she said. "And while she is too stinking cute, I wholeheartedly agree."

"The one with the unicorn?"

Rebecca nodded.

"That girl is going to keep us on her toes."

"Just as it should be."

Mandy's smile flashed, full and bright, and they spent another few minutes chatting, Rebecca getting the best foot massage ever, before she forced herself up from the table, slipped her protesting feet back into her heels, and waved goodbye.

"Stop wearing heels!" Mandy called as she pushed out of the PT Suite.

"Never—*oof*!"

She ran into a brick wall.

Or rather into a hockey player *built* like a brick wall.

Also known as . . . Kevin.

He raised a brow, one half of his mouth curving into a smirk that told her he'd overheard at least part of her conversation with Mandy. "Foot massage?"

"Spying?"

"I see you, babe, and I pay attention."

She narrowed her eyes. "If paying attention means eavesdropping."

And speaking of bright smiles flashing, Kevin's took her breath away. She knew it was comprised of six fake teeth from a puck gone awry in his rookie season, but he wasn't like some of the other guys who often went around sporting their gaps. He'd gotten those chompers repaired, and he was all that much hotter for it.

"Not gonna apologize, babe."

"I'm not your babe."

"God, you're fucking pretty when your eyes spark like that."

Her heart fluttered, but never one to allow herself to be thrown for a loop, Rebecca lifted her chin and pushed by him. Never mind that her thighs quivered and her pussy clenched. Never mind that she wanted to roll around in the spicy scent of him.

Nope. No way. No how.

"You forgot the part about useless and pathetic," she called over her shoulder.

And then she strode away, heels clicking on the floor, hips swaying perhaps more than was necessary.

"Babe." He caught her arm.

She teetered on her heels, not because he'd yanked or pushed or even grasped particularly hard.

Because he'd never touched her before.

Three years with the team.

Not one moment of contact.

And this . . . simply wrapping his fingers around the bare skin of her upper arm, calloused tips brushing along the inside of her bicep and making her shiver, and Rebecca threatened to turn stupid.

She'd been stupid before.

She couldn't afford to be stupid now.

"Let. Go."

He dropped his hand then lifted it again and steadied her when she immediately wavered on her feet.

"You okay?" he asked, brows drawn down, framing his gorgeous gray eyes.

The touch, the steadying, the gray eyes, and the concern on his face were the entire fucking problem. But fuck it all, she was a grown woman and she hadn't made it this far in her life by being a weakling, so she shook him off, stepped away, and lifted her chin.

"Fine." She started walking again. "Later."

Kevin caught up with her—not hard considering his legs might as well have been twice the length of hers. "Go out to dinner with me."

Not a question. And perhaps phrased like a request, though his tone screamed anything but. So, eavesdropping, contact that made her knees wobble, and now orders phrased as requests.

But still orders.

She circled back to the grown woman point she'd just been making to herself.

Because she was grown, and Kevin was not.

Thirty-four was leaps and bounds from twenty-four.

Ten whole years. A fucking decade, an entire generation. He'd been potty-training when she'd been in high school. Going to prom when she'd been getting divorced.

So, no.

The *boy* in front of her wasn't going to give her orders.

He stepped in front of her. "Bex. Dinner."

She rolled her eyes, moved around him. She had to dodge a very irritated-looking Gabe, the team's doctor, and the other Rebecca, or Nutritionist Rebecca, as the team had dubbed her, because she was in charge, as one might guess, of the players' nutrition program. They were having a heated discussion about something, but since Nutritionist Rebecca's conversations tended to trend that way, she kept moving and turned the corner.

Their conflict was easier to ignore than the two-hundred-pound elephant chasing her.

Especially when he said in that sexy voice of his, "Chicken?"

Her feet slid to a stop, heels *click-clacking* until silence filled the hall. Slowly, she spun to face him. "What did you say?"

That smile flashed again. "I asked if you were too chicken-shit to go on a date with me."

Red behind her eyes before her training took over—personal, business, who knew? For her, both of those worlds were the same. She had the team. The team was her life, and there wasn't room for anything, *anyone*, else in it.

That included twenty-four-year-old men.

And so, Rebecca unleashed a smile of her own.

Her shark smile.

Kevin, to his credit, didn't retreat like many a man before him. His expression smoothed out, caution entered his gaze. But his mouth didn't abide that caution.

"Burgers or pizza, sweetheart?"

Her vagina perked up. Fine, it had already been perked; it was on edge, practically ready to take over her brain and good sense and force her body to launch itself into Kevin's arms.

Instead of doing that, she spun back around and kept on walking. "Goodbye, Kevin."

He didn't stop her this time, but just before she turned the corner, he called. "I'm a professional athlete, babe. I don't stop when I see something I want."

"Put your hard work into something else, little boy."

Silence, and she breathed out a relieved breath when the door leading to the parking lot came into sight. Freedom.

"I'd rather put something into you, baby."

Rebecca froze, fingers on the handle, for a long moment before she was able to get herself into motion again.

Damn. The *little boy* was good.

Two

Kevin

It wasn't a trial to be sitting across the table from a beautiful woman.

Tall, gorgeous blue eyes, smile that was both mischievous and warm. In fact, the only problem with the entire scenario was the fact that the woman who he was sharing a meal with wasn't the one he'd had a flame for since the moment he'd laid eyes on her.

Namely, because if he held a torch for the woman across from him, he'd be a fucking pervert.

His mother reached over and fixed his hair.

Kevin was twenty-four.

Twenty-four.

And he still let his mom fix his hair.

Because she'd been through enough in her life that he wouldn't ever deny her something so simple and small, even if she made him feel ten years old in the process.

"I still can't believe you took the Cup to the Island on your day."

She was referring to the fact that the team had won it the

previous season, and tradition allowed for each of the guys—and girl—to spend a day with the huge trophy. Sometimes players took it home, others for a pool party, or maybe more notoriously to clubs or wild parties that involved keg stands—the last of which was no longer allowed because the Cup had been damaged. But Kevin hadn't wanted to do any of those things. In fact, he could think of nothing else but taking it to the Island, plunking it down on that rocky beach in front of the cabin, and cracking open a pair of beers.

One for him.

One for his dad . . . that his father could no longer drink.

He forced a smile, a pang echoing across his heart, but it was an old pain, more bittersweet than agony after all these years. His dad would have been proud, Kevin knew that, and winning it all was the dream he'd held on to from the moment he'd first watched a live hockey game at the age of five. To have the Cup his for a day was fucking amazing, and to be at the Island where the memories of his father were the strongest was its own special brand of remarkable.

It just couldn't be everything he'd imagined.

Because his dad hadn't been there.

"What'd you think I would do?" he asked his mother lightly.

She didn't miss a beat. "Fill it with beer and have a drinking contest."

He snorted. "Well, beer *was* involved."

A pat of his hand. "I'm glad you had that day." Her eyes told him she understood, that she wasn't hurt for not having been included in the outing. The Island had been his place with his dad, and he *had* stopped by her house before his time was up. "What were some of the other things the boys did?"

He grasped on to the change in topic and dished on a few of the other guys' adventures with the Cup, all of which were pretty tame when taking into account some of the things players of the past had done.

"No bonfires?" his mom asked with a smile.

"Not this time around."

"Probably for the best," she said. "I'm assuming the Cup's handlers frown on that sort of thing."

He took a swig of his beer. "You would be assuming right." A comfortable silence fell as their server approached, depositing their food in front of them. "How long are you in town?" he asked after their waitress had left.

His mom stilled, swallowing her bite of sandwich in a way that looked decidedly painful, but when she kept her eyes on her plate instead of looking up at him, Kevin's stomach twisted itself into knots.

Fuck.

"Mom—" He broke off. Was she sick? Was it bad? *Shit.* He didn't think he could handle losing another parent that way.

Warm fingers on his. "I'm sorry," she whispered. "I didn't realize what you might think. I'm fine."

His pulse slowed. "Are you sure?"

A nod. "I saw my doctor for my annual physical just before . . ."

That pause nearly killed him.

"Before what, Mom?"

She cleared her throat. "Just before I moved out here."

Kevin froze, relief pouring through him, and that loosened his tongue. "What the fuck, Mom? I thought you were dying, for God's sake." He shook his head. "How many times have I told you to come?"

"Watch your tongue, Kev," she said in a tone that was the reason he still let her fix his hair. Then she added, the words tinged with an acute pain that he knew all too well. "I wasn't ready before."

He turned his hand over, laced their fingers together. "I know."

His mother squeezed his hand, pulled back, and then blinked furiously before picking up her sandwich and taking another bite.

He copied her action, though the sub from one of his favorite places in the city suddenly tasted like ash. But as it often went with grief—or at least with his grief—the breath-stealing, sharp agony of remembrance only lasted a short while. Then it began fading, the pain easing, the tightness in his throat relaxing, even his taste buds returning to attention. After a few minutes, he could taste his sandwich again, could breathe normally, could focus on the woman in front of him.

"You need help selling the house, finding a place to stay?" he asked. "My spare room is ready and available until you do."

Her lips curved. "Always looking out for me, baby."

"You're my mom." She was his only family, the most important woman in his life, and he'd promised his dad he would never stop taking care of her.

"But no," she said. "I've already sold the house. It closed last week." She glanced down at her phone. "Whatever stuff I didn't donate or sell is on a truck and will be delivered to my apartment next Tuesday."

Kevin wasn't gonna lie. He stared at his mother for a good two minutes, shock having stolen his words. "Apartment?"

She smiled, and it was a gut-punch in the best way. He hadn't seen that smile in years. *In fucking years.* "It's amazing," she said, unlocking her phone and pulling up a dozen pictures. "It's in the cutest part of town and . . . get this! It's above a bookstore. Honestly, it couldn't be more perfect!"

His throat got tight again.

"And down the road is a farmer's market every Thursday and Sunday. Then there's the cutest little coffee shop a few doors down. It has the *best* lemon pound cake I've ever tasted in my life and—" He listened to her expound on the restaurants nearby, the park where she'd had a chance to pet not one but two pugs, and the floor-to-ceiling windows in her bedroom that gave her the perfect view of that park and even a sliver of the bay beyond. "—the best part is that it's close to you."

He pushed up from his chair, moved around the table, and

plunked down into the booth next to her, sliding an arm over her shoulders. Uncertainty was back in her eyes.

"It sounds perfect, Mom."

She relaxed.

"But you should have told me you were moving." He glared when she rolled her eyes. "You shouldn't have had to sort the house and move on your own."

Her shrug threatened to dislodge his arm. "I've been on my own for ten years now, bub. I'm used to it."

"You don't have to be." He dropped his arm when she shrugged again, knowing he was heavy and she was small, but he didn't move away. Instead, he nudged her shoulder with his and said, "Even if you *are* stubborn enough to be used to it."

She sighed. "I needed to do it on my own."

That he understood. "Okay, Mom, but you're staying at my place until your furniture comes."

A grin. "Why do you think you're buying me lunch?" He laughed as she shoved him out of the booth and gestured to his chair. "Now, get out of my booth, plunk your butt in that seat and finish your sandwich. I'll fix your favorite for dinner."

Knowing that meant biscuits along with chicken and dumplings, a meal that was decidedly off nutritionist-Rebecca's plan, but also one that he hadn't had in over a year, meant that Kevin hustled his ass into his chair and dove into his sandwich.

THREE

REBECCA

S he stared down the intern in front of her. The intern who'd just presented her with an extremely subpar representation of what she'd asked for.

"In what universe do you think this is acceptable?" she asked quietly, flipping the folder closed and reclining back in her desk chair.

The little man-child spread his legs, reclining back into his own far more uncomfortable wooden chair, and adopted the persona of a horribly wronged individual by crossing his arms and releasing a long-suffering sigh. "You didn't give me enough time."

Rebecca slipped her feet back into her heels, stood, and picked up the folder. "You want to rethink that excuse?"

A huff was her only response.

"So, I *didn't* see you at Trent's last night? Downing beer way past midnight with a group of fellow frat boys instead of completing the project I asked you for?" She shoved the folder back at him, smirking when he struggled to catch it before it hit the floor and stand at the same time.

His brows drew together. "Where do you get off spying on me?"

She lifted one red-painted fingernail. "First, I happen to like to get a drink after work every once in a while. Second, when that drink is with one Devon Scott"—her former boss and owner of the premier sports management group in the nation—"and I know my intern would like to make the leap to that field, I pay the fuck attention. And so does Devon. So, when my intern is making a fucking nuisance of himself at the bar, coming on too strong with the waitresses, arguing about paying the tab he racked up at the end of the night, tipping over chairs in a drunken stupor, and well, just being your own special brand of asshole, I pay even more attention." She paused, took in his pale face, dropped her tone conspiratorially. "And then, when my intern doesn't turn in the work I asked for in a quality I expect . . . that means I hand him his final check and advise him to get his shit together so he doesn't find every door in this industry firmly shut to him."

She handed him the envelope with his final check, opened the door to the hallway, and waited.

Then waited some more.

"This is when you go," she prompted.

He got up, all bravado and righteous anger gone, and escaped into the hall.

"Fuck boys," she muttered. "The lot of them."

"Me, too?"

Her heart skipped a beat when she turned and saw Kevin. He was grinning and so fucking gorgeous it took her breath away. Wide shoulders, slender hips, those gorgeous gray eyes, and an ass she could bounce a dime off of.

Not that she'd looked.

Fuck, who was she kidding? *Of course* she'd looked.

"Dinner?" he asked, lips twitching.

She didn't bother answering. This particular exchange had been going on for the last two weeks anytime she was in her office at the arena. He'd seek her out with a "PR issue" or bump into her—which she thought was really him trying to pretend to not be seeking her out—and he'd always ask the same one-word question.

Dinner?

No, she couldn't fucking go to dinner.

He was young and successful and way too pretty to be a hockey player—not that she'd tell him that because the last thing he needed was a confidence boost or God forbid that she admit she was attracted to him and he found more ways to *bump* into her. But the point was that she was old, didn't shit where she ate, and more than either of those things . . . she was broken.

Inside, she was broken.

So, no men.

And definitely, no men who might mean something.

But most especially no beautiful, lovely, *nice* men who were just beginning their upward climb. Men who had their whole lives in front of them. Men who didn't need a woman to hold them back, but to lift them up and support them and give them a family.

She couldn't do that.

And it hurt.

Fuck, it hurt.

Almost two decades since she'd found out that she couldn't have babies, and while she'd locked that desire down, pushed away thoughts of carrying a life in her womb, of cradling a newborn in her arms, this man threatened that. She'd shoved her fantasies into a mental chest, chained it closed, slapped a dozen locks on it, then had thrown their keys in just as many directions.

But two weeks of Kevin—hell, she was pathetic enough to remember *each* of the twelve times he'd asked her out to dinner—and the chains on that chest were weakening.

Rather than being happy and fulfilled with her career, with her exorbitant hourly rate to keep her company instead of a husband and baby, she was acutely aware all over again of what she would never have. With just twelve one-word questions and a few sharp—on her end—and teasing—on his—conversations, everything was coming apart at the seams.

This man was dangerous to her mental well-being.

She barely knew him and yet . . . he made her feel. Worse, he made her want.

She couldn't want.

She couldn't.

"No to dinner."

Her first mistake was her tone. It revealed too damned much. Her second was not pushing Kevin away when he touched her. But his fingers on her jaw felt good, his calloused skin brushing along her throat, making her shiver. That, paired with his gentle question, was her undoing.

"You okay?"

Oh fuck.

Her eyes filled with tears and she spun away, darting into her office before they escaped, slamming the door in his face so he wouldn't see. Unfortunately, he caught the panel before she could close it completely then slipped inside, took one look at her face, and shut it behind him.

Then he reached for her.

And she let him.

Fuck, but she let him.

It was fucking incredible.

Strong arms wrapped tightly around her, and Rebecca found herself with a nose full of Kevin's spicy scent, her cheek pressed flat to his hard chest, words of comfort rumbling through the wide expanse to reach her ears.

Not that she could decipher them.

Because she was crying, sobbing like an absolute idiot and unable to stop, and she hadn't cried in going on ten years, not since her parents had passed and she'd lost the last bit of softness in her soul.

Her parents were what brought her out of herself.

She shoved hard at Kevin's chest, throat tightening all over again when it seemed like he wouldn't let her go. But then he did and she stepped back, trying to ignore the smear of makeup and red lipstick on the soft gray of his T-shirt, which she was also trying to ignore was almost the exact same shade as his eyes.

Eyes she couldn't face.

"Baby—"

She spun away, walking around her desk to begin digging through the drawers for her emergency makeup kit. Based on the amount of product on his shirt, she'd need the full shebang. Ignoring the two-hundred-and-twenty-pound elephant in the room, along with the fact that she'd just used the word *shebang*, Rebecca located her case and sat down at her desk to fix her face.

Her mask. Her shield from the world.

Whatever.

"Sweetheart—"

"I'm on my period," she blurted and then did her level best to not look at him when the only thing that greeted her in response was absolute silence.

Her best wasn't good enough because her eyes drifted up . . . and collided with storm clouds.

Kevin raised a brow.

Her gaze darted back to her makeup. Wipes, primer, foundation, mascara, liner, eye shadow, lipstick, eyebrow pencil. She lined them all up precisely on her desk.

"I'll buy you a new shirt," she muttered, "but I'd appreciate you don't tell the guys about this."

More silence. Then footsteps. "Don't tell the guys you're not actually superhuman?" A beat. "Contrary to what you might think, they already know that." He plunked into the chair her pathetic intern Colby had just vacated. "You shouldn't have brought us brownies, Killer."

She lifted a brow, even though it was only partially redrawn in, and despite herself, her lips twitched. "Killer?"

"The team knows you well," was all he said.

Killer. She snorted, not admitting to the fact aloud, even though she tucked that gem close to her heart. Was it seriously fucked up that she loved they'd given her a nickname *and* that it was something like Killer? "I protect what's mine."

One half of his mouth curved up. "Yeah, we know."

"And we bow to the goddess under pain of brownies," he teased.

"You mean under pain of not getting them," she said then sighed. "I know what you're doing."

His brow rose.

"I know you're not talking about brownies."

He sprawled in the chair, legs spreading, back hitting the cushions, confidence exuding from every pore. "*I* know you're not on your period."

She'd had a sentence on the tip of her tongue, but his reply had that poofing off into a cloud of smoke. Most men ran at the first mention of menstruation, didn't bring it up again. "Oh?" she asked in a dangerous tone as she fixed her liner. "How do you figure?"

Kevin leaned forward to rest his elbows on her desk. "Because you had your period two weeks ago."

Rebecca froze, liner an inch from her eye, and slowly glanced up from the pocket-sized mirror on her desk to meet his gaze. Then she showed her hand. She knew she shouldn't have, but she was too taken aback because . . . how could he possibly know that?

"You always bring brownies when you're on your period."

Her mouth dropped open.

How. In. The. Fuck. Could. He. Know. That?

How did he know that she always made a triple batch of double chocolate chip brownies on the first day of her period because cramps and losing one's uterine lining necessitated having copious amounts of chocolate at hand . . . but also that she always brought the majority of the brownies to the rink because if she actually ate three batches, she would never fit into her clothes.

And she fucking loved her clothes.

Hence that exorbitant hourly rate.

"So," he said when she forced herself to keep going with her makeup. "Not hormones, but still upset. Do I need to go and destroy that little . . . fuck boy? Was that what you called him?"

"Yes," she said. "That was what he was, and no. I took care of him already, no assault charges necessary."

"Damn," he said. "Taking away my fun."

"Well, your *fun* would involve me pulling overtime in order to spin it, so I'd rather you didn't."

"Fine." He rapped his knuckles on the edge of her desk. "But only if you go out to dinner with me."

She swept on some eye shadow then proceeded with her lipstick, ignoring him.

"You know," he murmured. "Watching you put on your makeup may be the sexiest thing I've ever seen." He stood, moved around the desk then dropped to his haunches, turning her chair to place and caging her in. Rebecca's breath caught, and he noticed. He *knew* she was attracted to him.

Dangerous.

This man was so fucking dangerous.

"I need makeup to cover up my wrinkles."

A blurt, a horrible one that was made strictly out of desperation, but Kevin's reaction wasn't anything she could have ever anticipated.

He grinned and swept a finger across her cheekbone. "Well, I happen to like my women with a few lines."

She gasped, outraged, and slapped his hand away. "Y-you—"

He broke into peals of laughter, huge guffaws that washed over her and soon had her lips tugging upward. Then she was laughing, too, enjoying the lightness after her dark thoughts of ten minutes before.

Yes, sharing a moment of amusement with this man wasn't horrible.

Their laughter faded, and he patted her knee and stood. "I'll pick you up for dinner after practice. Six thirty work for you?"

"I didn't agree to dinner," she said, heart skipping a beat as he swaggered toward the door.

"I also didn't agree to not tell the boys you've been making us period brownies all this time."

She narrowed her eyes, gritted out, "You wouldn't."

He grinned, hand on the doorknob. "I'm also going to go discreetly change my shirt and not answer any questions about whose makeup is smeared across my chest."

"Kevin—"

"Italian good?" He paused on the threshold, waited.

"Period or not, you owe me chocolate gelato."

A sexy smile. "Deal."

Then he was gone, and Rebecca was alone, her tube of Dior Rouge No. 999 dangling from her fingertips.

She'd cried.

And agreed to dinner.

What in the fuck was happening with her life?

Four

Kevin

He could barely concentrate on the drills, and Blue knew it. "What the fuck, dude?" his linemate hissed when they reset for the third time because Kevin had screwed up the path he was supposed to be skating.

"Sorry," he muttered, shutting off the parts of his brain that weren't devoted to hockey, compartmentalizing the memory of seeing, *of feeling* a woman he'd never thought of as anything but steel and hard edges fall apart in his arms.

He'd hoped that there might be something soft beneath that armor.

He'd just never expected broken.

Or his desire to step in and take all of those hurts away.

He wasn't a white knight. He definitely didn't get his kicks by swooping in and saving women. But Rebecca was different.

From the first moment he'd laid eyes on her, Kevin had known she was different.

He'd wanted to get to know that different.

And while a weeping female might normally turn him off,

when that vulnerability was in the form of Rebecca, he wanted to—

The whistle trilled.

He got his shit together, pushed everything aside except for hockey, and *moved*. The ice crunched beneath his skates as he sprinted for the corner, slipping neatly in front of the defensemen and scooping up the puck. He passed it over to Blue, sprinted to the front of the net. But he wasn't there to score. Kevin was a distraction, and he played his part well, jostling with the other defensemen before sliding back enough that Blue passed the puck off and then took his place.

A quick shot. A pop as Blue deflected it down and low and far side—

"Fuck," Brit hissed as it slid home.

Blue grinned. Kevin just breathed a little easier at not having fucked up.

His heroic goal—though he hated when anyone referred to it as that because it had been the entire team who'd won the Cup, not just him and one moment—had secured him his first legit contract. He'd gotten long-term and big money.

And the security of knowing that he'd be in San Francisco for a long time, or eight more years, at least.

Now it was time to make those eight years count. To stop waiting for his life to begin, for the other shoe to drop.

It was time to live.

Hopefully, with a certain brunette with gorgeous chocolate eyes and an affinity for fire engine red lipstick and nail polish.

"Gotcha," Blue teased Brit.

"Should have known you'd go far side," she grumbled but tapped Blue on the shin guards with her stick. "Good one." She poked Kevin. "Especially with this one's wide ass blocking my view."

"I'll have you know that I'm perfectly petite," he said, lips twitching.

"For a two-hundred-and-twenty-pound lightweight? Yeah, definitely *petite*."

"One might even say—"

"A couple more times, boys," Todd called. He was one of their assistant coaches and focused primarily on offense. "Then we'll call it a day."

They cut the banter and got to work.

Kevin loved the game, lived, and breathed the sport, but it was also his job and that meant focusing when he'd rather be down the hall pressing his advantage with Rebecca. It also meant going to practice, pulling his head out of his ass, and getting his shit together so he wasn't the weakest link on the team.

After which it meant being stopped for a quick interview two steps off the ice by a local blogger who'd been one of the earliest supporters of the team. Then being pulled aside to review some tape of his skating—his weakest part of the game.

"See? There?" Steph said. She was a former figure skater and one of the most sought-after skating coaches in the NHL. The Gold had been lucky enough to get her on the payroll because one of their defensemen, Mike Stewart, was married to a former gold medalist and Sara Stewart, née Jetty, had competed with her in the same circuits. "You're relying on your inside edge too much. If you can trust that outside edge more, your transition will be smoother and faster. It'll save you time and you can get your ass back sooner, which I think Brit will appreciate."

Kevin grinned. "I think you're right. Got some drills for me?"

"Emailed already. And I'll see you on-ice tomorrow at ten."

He nodded, thanking her, hating the idea of skating drills even more than practice drills, even while understanding that they were a necessary evil and that his game would be all the better for it.

But . . . he'd heard his entire life what a shitty skater he was, and he'd made it to the NHL despite that fact.

So, you think you're too much of a hotshot to be coached now?

It was his dad's voice he heard when he was being unreasonable.

Or if not unreasonable, then at least not in the right headspace.

The truth was that he'd always struggled to focus on drills and practice and repetition and repetition and repetition. Games had been his bread and butter, allowing for freedom and creativity and to just be swept up in the action.

Lucky that he'd been drafted by a team that allowed for that.

The Gold played a definite system, but it wasn't so stringent that it didn't allow for improvisation.

Kevin didn't know what he'd do without that freedom.

Well, he *did* know that he certainly wouldn't have been able to stomach the notion of an hour of skating drills in the morning if it hadn't been there.

Steph tucked the tablet under her arm and waved, striding down the hall and pausing at the door to the locker room to holler, "Mika, Tal, Brian. Stop by my office before you leave."

Silence as she strode on before a trio of groans drifted into the hall.

She turned back to Kevin and winked. "Music to my ears."

He snorted, shaking his head. "I'll see you tomorrow." A beat. "Without the groaning."

"Get it all out today," she teased as she disappeared around the corner.

He shook his head again then walked into the locker room and got down to the business of changing. If his inclination was right, then Rebecca would be regretting her agreement to dinner and be actively planning her escape.

Not to worry, he had plans in place to stop that from happening.

In the form of one nearly six-foot-tall blond beauty.

Brit raised a brow when he passed her stall and sat down at the bench in front of his. But instead of shaking his head as he'd done every day for the past two weeks, he allowed the barest hint of a smile to slip out, along with a nod.

"Really?" she mouthed.

"Really," he mouthed back. "So, little help?"

"On it." She stood, shrugged into her suit jacket and crossed to him. "Wash really good, Kev. Don't want to blow this one."

"Noted," he muttered.

"And wine. She likes red wine."

Of course she did. He nodded his thanks at his teammate and set about the business of washing off the hockey stink and wrestling himself into something presentable.

Or at least not nose-wrinkling.

Because he'd waited more than three years for this chance and wasn't going to fuck it up.

FIVE

REBECCA

She smelled a rat.

A lovely, very talented rat, but a rat nonetheless.

"And then I thought that with the clothing offer coming in, I could use someone to help me overhaul my social media," Brit said, sprawling into Rebecca's desk chair. "I'm shit at it, and part of my contract with them is a certain amount of posts . . ."

She went on about engagement and hashtags and scheduling posts to hit a target demographic.

All things that would normally be Rebecca's kryptonite, or maybe the surefire way to get her to orgasm.

But . . . the rat.

Especially when Brit had snagged Rebecca by the arm as she'd headed out of her office, drawing her away from Gabe and Nutritionist Rebecca, locked in another typically tense conversation in the hall, before hauling her back into her office, shoving her down into her expensive desk chair, and then had taken up her current position.

Read: blocking Rebecca's planned escape.

She should have left earlier, but she'd gotten caught up watching practice, under the guise of fixing her fuck boy of an intern's subpar social media example posts, and had taken way too many stills of a certain player she'd sobbed on—fuck her life—and had been obsessed with since the first moment she'd seen him without a shirt.

Fucking twenty-four years old.

And fucking gorgeous.

A smattering of chest hair, pecs that were perfectly squeezable, abs that were defined into perfect squares she was desperate to trace with her tongue.

She was around gorgeous athletes day in and day out. Thus, the sight of a six-pack shouldn't have made her cream herself.

But Kevin's six-pack?

That was different.

However, he'd also only been twenty-one then, more lean lines and lanky strength than the solid man he was now. So, she'd shoved that attraction down, had forced herself to be content with burning up the battery on her vibrator.

Then the big win at the end of the season, followed by his words on the bench.

I. Want. You.

She still thought about the raspy way he'd told her that, how his gray eyes had flashed with lightning, how her breath had caught, and her thighs clenched. It had been the first time ever she'd felt incapable of strutting away in her four-inch heels and, namely, that had been because her knees had wobbled.

Now his hot stare seemed to follow her everywhere.

Worse?

She found that she liked it.

And she really shouldn't.

" . . . I don't know a thing about demographics or—"

There was a knock at the door, and Rebecca would have had

to be completely dense to miss the relieved expression on Brit's face. Her friend popped to her feet and opened the door. To no one's surprise in the room, Kevin strolled into the office.

He didn't say anything, his gray gaze locked onto her, studying her closely for a long moment before Brit pulled out her phone.

"Oh, that's Stefan. I'll . . . catch you later, Rebecca."

Then she was through the door, and they were alone.

Her office never normally seemed small, but with Kevin inside of it, watching her so intently, she found that all the air in the space had disappeared.

"You're feeling better," he said, crossing over to her and leaning back against the desk. In front of her, mere inches away, sucking up even more air, making every nerve on her body stand up and take notice.

"I'm always fine." She closed a folder, stood.

Kevin didn't move, and instantly she regretted her decision to move.

He'd been close before but now, barely a piece of paper could fit between them. "You're not," he murmured, tucking a strand behind her ear that had her stifling a shiver. "And that's okay." Fingers along the underside of her jaw. "No one is okay all of the time."

She swallowed hard, stared at him unblinking for a moment before she remembered herself. "Well"—another swallow—"I should go." Nudging the chair back with her foot, she started to slip past him. "I've got a busy night ahead and—"

He caught her arm.

"I think you're forgetting something?"

"Nope," she said. "I've just got a lot of work and—"

"You need to eat," he said. "And I seem to remember you promising to do that with me."

In cases like this, there was only one course of action.

To play dumb.

"Nope," she replied. "I don't remember that at all. In fact"—she snatched up a file at random—"I've got a slammed evening ahead of me, so you'd better leave me to it."

Lie.

Total lie.

She was ahead of work and with the season not yet underway, that workload was light. Something she suspected he most definitely knew, based on the way those gray eyes pinned her in place.

Pulse pounding, it was difficult to maintain eye contact.

But she was Rebecca Fucking Stravokraus. So despite the lie, despite the urge to look away—or worse to launch herself into his arms and taste that fucking glorious mouth instead of sobbing against that equally glorious chest—she stiffened her spine and kept her eyes on his.

After a long moment, he released her.

And no, that wasn't disappointment she felt.

Certainly not.

No freaking way.

Down that path led insanity, and Rebecca did *not* do insanity.

But Kevin didn't leave. He spun around and gathered up all the files on her desk, bent and scooped up her ridiculously expensive but amazing red Michael Kors bag, shoved the papers inside.

"You can work at dinner."

Then he took her arm and started to lead her to the door.

Two steps in, he stopped and stared down at her feet, one half of his mouth curving.

He dropped her arm again, walked back to her desk, and snatched up her heels then crossed back to her, crouched down, and in some ridiculously sexy and totally insane version of Cinderella, helped her step into them.

And she let him.

Didn't make a peep, just let him put on her heels, wrap his hand around her upper arm, and lead her from her office.

She didn't say anything when he paused to flick off the light, to shut the door.

Not one word when he led her out of the rink and into the parking lot.

Never in her life had she been completely mute, never had she gone along without a fight, never had she let a man lead her around by her arm.

But Kevin . . . he was different, wasn't he?

Still didn't mean she wasn't herself and so, by the time he'd opened the passenger's side door on his sleek black sedan, she'd regained at least a semblance of her personality.

She side-stepped the opening, reached for her bag.

He held it out of her reach, looked deeply into her eyes again, and shook his head, a slow, sexy smile curving his mouth.

"Dinner, beautiful," he said softly. "Is that such a trial?"

Then he rounded his car, opened his own door, and got inside. She noticed that he tucked her bag—with her keys and wallet and all the files from her desk inside—on the outside of his leg. And while there was only a file or two that could use her eyes that night, the rest of the items proved more problematic.

Hard to escape sans keys.

"I'm—"

"I'll let you pick the wine," he cajoled. "Cab? Merlot? Pinot Noir?"

She could almost taste a really good Cabernet on her tongue, could definitely picture him staring at her with warm eyes as he poured her a glass, studying her as she drank, or maybe sharing the glass with her, his mouth touching the same spot on the glass as hers did . . . and then maybe touching hers without the excuse of a glass.

"Just dinner, baby. One meal."

Rebecca hesitated.

Such a slippery slope this was, and yet . . . fuck did she want to go out to dinner with him, to have just a few moments alone with this wonderful, beautiful man before she had to cut her losses and run.

To that end, she sucked in a breath, dropped into the passenger's seat, and closed the door.

She almost didn't hear the relieved sigh cross Kevin's lips.

But she did.

And that little puff of air made her heart skip a beat.

Because for whatever insane reason, he wanted to spend time with her, too.

Six

KEVIN

He was fucking it up.

Brit had been the best wingman he could ask for and—

"Will you turn on the radio?"

He cut his eyes to the right. "So you can ignore me?" The light turned red and he slid to a stop, twisting to face her fully.

"You're doing a damned good job of that already," she said. "We've been sitting in silence for fifteen minutes. At least this way, I'd get to have something to fill the empty space."

Kevin winced at the sharp words, though she wasn't wrong in the least.

Hence the fucking things up. He'd been trying to come up with something to say that wasn't fucking stupid.

What's up? Dumb. *How's work?* Also, fucking dumb. *You look beautiful.* What was she supposed to say to that? *I've been fantasizing about having you in my car, my space for three years, and now I don't know what I could have been possibly thinking because you are way the fuck out of my league?*

Truth. But also both stalkerish and supremely pathetic.

So silence.

Which was just as bad as all of those combined.

"You're right," he admitted.

One brow lifted. "I'm right?"

He shrugged. "Yes." The light turned green and he acceler-ated, keeping his eyes on the road as he admitted, "I'm nervous."

"*I* make *you* nervous?"

She sounded so absolutely incredulous that he couldn't help but laugh. "Baby, I've seen guys' balls shrivel up into walnuts from one glimpse of those gorgeous chocolate eyes."

Silence.

Then a look very similar to the one he'd just described, but instead of making his balls crawl up into his body, Kevin's dick twitched. He'd always loved that razor-sharp slice, the fire beneath the surface, and the way she didn't take any shit.

"And *your* balls?"

A grin. "Right where they're supposed to be."

"Probably because they're so big," she muttered.

He snorted. *She* snorted. Then they were both laughing and that was so much better than the uncomfortable silence of the previous minutes. Because Rebecca wasn't afraid to speak her mind, to demand something more.

God, he liked this woman.

"Okay," he said, once his laughter had subsided. "Let's start with the easy stuff. Favorite color. Go."

There that brow went again, and though she didn't say the *"Really?"* aloud, that curve of her eyebrow said it clearly enough.

"Yes, really," he replied.

A sigh then, "Gold."

Now it was his turn for a brow.

"Yes, really," she countered. "I can't help it. I love sparkly things. And just to continue this ridiculous conversation, what's yours?"

"Pink."

Her jaw dropped open, and he smirked. "Kidding. I'm actually more of a lavender guy or maybe periwinkle."

She pulled out her phone, started scrolling through it, and he might have been insulted that she was so effectively ignoring him, if not for the fact that she said, "Aha!" and then shoved the screen in his face for a second before pulling it back. "Blue. I knew it. So cliché."

Kevin snorted. "You got me."

"I also know your favorite food, favorite movie, and whether you prefer the mountains or the ocean." A smile that slid down his spine. "I know all the boys' favorites."

"Hmm." He turned right, sliding into a tiny parking lot, and squeezing his car into one of the spots. "So, you know all. Now you've got to share."

She froze. "I hardly know all."

"You know blue, lasagna, *Die Hard*, and that I'd love to live on the beach." A shrug. "You know all."

Her cell slipped back into her purse, silence for a long moment as she seemed to be weighing her options. "Fine. But just so we're equal. You know gold, pasta carbonara, *Caddyshack*, and definitely the beach."

"Mmm," he said. "Tiny string bikinis."

The strangest expression crossed her face, but it was gone so fast that he almost thought he could have imagined that sliver of pain. But when it disappeared, her lips tipped up into a sexy smile. "Yes. Definitely teeny, tiny bikinis." She popped the door, started to push out.

He slipped his fingers around her wrist, stayed her motion. "You don't have to dish, but"—his other hand cupped her jaw— "you also don't have to hide, sweetheart."

"I'm not hiding."

"You're really good at hiding, baby," he said. "But I see it." He released her. "Still doesn't mean you have to share."

Her lips parted, tongue darting out to moisten the bottom

one, and Kevin could have sworn he felt that flash of damp, pink heat on his cock. "I don't know what you're talking about."

"Don't you?" he asked, eyes locked with hers.

And the shadows in the depths of her chocolate ones told him that, yes, she *did* know exactly what he was talking about.

"In your own time," he murmured.

"In my own time, what?"

"Sharing," he told her. "Pasta and movie preferences aside, it's all on your terms, baby." He opened his own door, sliding out and crossing around to hold open hers. He didn't step back when she stood, hesitated, then ultimately slipped past him. Kevin would have been a fucking liar if he'd denied inhaling as she'd moved, soaking in some of the scent that was uniquely Rebecca's.

Cinnamon with a hint of sweetness.

The perfect manifestation of the woman in front of him.

He caught her hand as she started striding for the restaurant, lacing their fingers together. "Just so I know in order to fill our awkward silence on the way back to the rink, what's your favorite type of music?"

She turned, glanced up at him, mouth twitching. "Are you sure you want to know?"

He stilled. "Is it that bad?"

"There's a reason that Brit and I get along so well."

A groan. "Boy bands?" The starting goalie was well-known for her affinity for the male-dominated groups and tormented the team often when it was her turn to control the playlist.

Those fucking songs were catchy and as a result, Kevin often found himself humming them well into practice and the evening.

A fact he was taking to his death bed.

She patted his chest. "Don't worry," she said. "I've got you covered. Brit stole her playlist from me."

"No," he said. "No way. I'm not—"

They'd reached the door, but before he could open it for her, she snagged the handle and pulled. Soft music filled the space, one of his favorite Italian places in the city. There were maybe ten tables inside, and it could fit a max of thirty people, but the pasta was fresh, the wine was local and off the charts, and the atmosphere was relaxed.

No need for a suit and tie, but no strange looks if he wore one.

Kevin didn't mind wearing suits. It was just that he was required to wear them for games and events and fundraisers, and by the time all was said and done, it seemed that he wore little else.

So not being required to wear one, but also not being out of place wearing one, was the ultimate win-win for him when it came to post-game pasta cravings.

"Kev!" Vivian said. "I haven't seen you in a few weeks."

"My mom's been in town and keeping me busy."

"Busy that didn't involve me?" Vivian plunked her hands onto her ample hips, red curly ponytail bouncing as she moved.

"Unfortunately, yes," he said. "She's been running me ragged and cooking enough food while staying at my place that the team's nutritionist would lose her shit if she knew."

Rebecca coughed, or maybe that was her smothering a laugh because she murmured, "Don't make me confess all to the other Rebecca."

Kevin snorted. "That's blackmail."

"You know it."

He turned to her, brushed his knuckles across her cheek. "Will it make things better if I agree to the playlist?"

She pondered that for a moment then nodded slowly. "Yes. Yes, it will." A beat. "So long as the pasta carbonara is fabulous."

He turned to Vivian. "What do you think, Vivi? Can you promise fabulous carbonara?"

"Is my hair red?" She laughed, picked up two menus, and nodded to the table in the back. "Or it used to be anyway. Go on and take your usual spot. I'll bring you some waters and flatware."

"Thanks." He squeezed Rebecca's hand, led her to his favorite booth.

"So, here's another getting to know you question," he said when they'd reached the table. "Left or right-handed?"

She rolled her eyes. "I'm discovering that I know so much more than you, leftie."

He gently bumped his shoulder against hers, loving that she was only a few inches shorter than him in those sexy as fuck heels. "You spied on me with that questionnaire."

Silence.

"It's not from the questionnaire." Her cheeks flared, and she quickly looked away, sliding into the booth.

"Oh?" He sat next to her, ignoring her protest, running a finger across the bright red flush on either cheekbone. "So, how'd you know?"

Her shoulders stiffened. "I know everything about the team."

He might have believed that if he hadn't been sitting so close, but he *was* sitting close, and because of that, he saw the lie flash across her eyes. "No," he murmured, sliding closer because he couldn't stop himself. Her thigh was flush against his and while it was fucking glorious, he didn't let the gloriousness of it distract him from the truth. "That's not it. Try again."

Vivian came over then, plunking down the menus and a couple of waters in front of them. "Do you want something to drink?"

"I'll take a Cabernet," Rebecca said. "Thank you."

"Make it a good one," he teased, earning a smack on the arm from Vivian.

"You know all of my wines are fabulous."

"Part of the reason I've brought Rebecca here," he said. "I've been assured that the way to her heart is through a really good red wine."

Rebecca snorted, but Vivian grinned. "Well, lucky for you, I *do* have a really good red wine." A beat. "You want to share? Or your usual."

"My usual. Thanks."

She nodded. "Bring your mama by next week. Give her a night off from cooking."

"Deal."

Another nod. "Now, do you want a few more minutes with the menu? Or should I just skip the formalities and bring a lasagna and pasta carbonara?"

"Carbonara sounds perfect," Rebecca said.

"Bread?"

"The more carbs, the better."

Vivian reached across the table and squeezed Rebecca's hand. "Woman after my own heart," she said. "Make sure to save room for tiramisu."

"That sounds glorious."

"It is." Vivian patted her hips. "My Robbie's cooking is why I've given up on wearing a smaller pants size. I can't resist it and—"

Robbie came up just then, slipping a hand around Vivian's waist and kissing her neck. "I love you just the way you are, my love. Now, let's leave the two lovebirds to their meal." He started to tug her away.

"I'll be right back with the wine—" She bustled away, and Robbie winked at them and shook his head, mouthing, "No, she won't," before taking her hand and tugging her through the swinging door into the kitchen.

"I think I love them," Rebecca murmured.

"I know I do."

They'd all but adopted him from the moment he'd first stepped through the door to their restaurant. He'd eaten more meals here than his own kitchen, spent more quiet nights here away from his empty apartment, dawdling over a glass of beer, not wanting to be alone and finding that with Robbie and Vivian pausing at his table, shoving morsels of food onto his plate for his "approval" that life as a young twenty-something in a big city, on a new team seemed much less lonely when he was there.

Rebecca glanced down at her hands, quiet for a long moment before a slow, shuddering breath seemed to escape her.

"They remind me of my parents."

And that was the moment he realized that he wasn't the only one who was lonely.

SEVEN

REBECCA

S tupid. So fucking stupid.

Why had she said that?

She barely thought about her parents or her past or the fact that she'd spent more than a decade of her life in hospitals —first as a patient and then as a visitor and caregiver to her mother . . . then her father.

Gone now.

Them. The person she'd been.

Her old life.

Kevin shifted slightly, those gray eyes locking onto hers, and he didn't ask anything inane, as she'd half expected a man of his age to. Something along the lines of: *Oh, do they cook, too?* Or perhaps: *Do they work together also?*

Instead, he just studied her closely and asked, "How so?"

She couldn't hold on to his gaze, found her eyes drifting down to her nails, to the slightest chip in her gel manicure. She'd need to squeeze in time to get them redone this week before the travel and workload made it virtually impossible to schedule a full hour for something as unimportant as her nails.

But they were important to her. She liked them to look put together. In fact, she preferred for her entire exterior to appear put together.

It was easier to patch up the cracks that way.

People didn't look too closely if the exterior was without flaws.

Except Kevin.

And once again, she was reminded of how dangerous he was.

Especially when he allowed the silence to stretch between them, nodding in thanks when a server—not Vivian, Rebecca noted—came by with her wine and his beer. He simply kept his thigh pressed to hers, the warmth of his leg not oppressive and yet also not fading into the background, not letting her off the hook.

Time.

He was giving her the gift of time . . . and patience.

She wondered how long that patience would last if she deliberately avoided answering the question he so obviously wanted an answer to, how long that affable attitude would last when she didn't give him what he wanted. When, instead of giving him the chase, the carrot at the end of the fishing pole, if she only gave him what she allowed him to have.

"How did you find this place?" she asked, shifting in the booth so their legs no longer touched but playing it off by rotating so she faced him more fully.

He mirrored her movement. "I live in the neighborhood."

"Oh?"

"You didn't know that?" he teased.

She hadn't known that. Well, she had she supposed. Or *could* have because she had all of the players' addresses, but that was a piece of information she tended to only access when it was fully necessary.

Read: when PR emergencies demanded she show up on their doorstep.

Which was usually trailed by a verbal reaming that shaped them up in one visit.

But Kevin hadn't had any PR emergencies. He went to practice, showed up for games, didn't get into trouble at clubs or run wild through the city's female populace. He was her model player —studied the sound bites, was always open for an interview, and never anything but courteous.

He played the game to perfection.

Except with her.

Except . . . maybe with her, too. Because despite her misgivings, she was sitting in a booth next to him about to share a meal.

He rested his arm on the back of the booth, fingers so close to her nape that her skin prickled and she found herself shifting slightly, the intent to move away, and yet somehow finding that she'd actually eliminated the distance between her skin and his hand.

Her reward was the lightest brush of those calloused fingertips on her neck before they captured a strand of her hair between his thumb and forefinger and began to absently roll it.

One way. Then the other. One way. Then the other.

She shivered.

His expression told her he knew why, but he didn't stop the action, just kept rolling that bit of hair between his fingers, heat rapidly trailing the shivers. Rebecca swallowed hard, shifting in her seat in an effort to ease the ache between her thighs and hoping all the while that he didn't understand what she was doing.

Probably too much to ask, based on the mischievousness in his eyes.

But he didn't comment on her thigh clenching or the goose bumps prickling to life on her skin. Instead, he kept his hand in place and . . . gave.

"My dad died before I made it into the NHL. I'd been scouted, offers in the works, but he never saw it become official." A sigh. "For a long time, I fought and scrounged to make it into the league because it was so damned important to him, because he sacrificed so much for my training, because I knew he'd have loved nothing more than me making it to the highest level." Her breath caught when his fingers released the strand and his warm palm cupped the back of her neck. "Then I finally made the team, finally had a starting position, and . . ."

"What?"

"I found I didn't know what the hell I was doing or who the hell I was doing it for."

Her brows drew down.

"I know it doesn't make sense—"

"No," she murmured. "It makes sense. When you live your life for other people for too long, you almost forget to know what *you* want, what kind of person you are inside. It's like the version of yourself that you present to the world is only two-dimensional, and it's a real struggle to become fully fledged again." She bit her lip. "You've focused for so long on simply keeping your head down, on surviving and just pushing through to the end that . . ."

"You forget who you are."

She nodded.

Their food appeared at that moment, and it was probably a good thing because Rebecca didn't know what else she could have said in that moment.

She probably would have just blurted, "You're twenty-four. *Twenty-four!* How could you know that?" And yet, she was beginning to understand how unfair it was for her to misjudge Kevin just because he was younger than her. So instead, she said, "I'm guessing that Robbie's lasagna helped you find yourself again?"

He grinned. "Not really. Though the homemade noodles, sauce, and ricotta are akin to a religious experience. It was more like they saw I was alone and lost then firmly tugged me into their circle."

"That sounds lovely."

"It was fucking incredible."

Her heart skipped a beat at the sincerity in his words. She took a bite of the carbonara, closed her eyes as the flavors coalesced into bliss on her tongue. "All in all, based on the food alone, it seems like a lucky place to be tugged into."

"Definitely." He cut into his lasagna, scooped up a bite onto his fork.

"What happened to your dad?" she asked softly.

And he gave again. "Heart attack. I was fourteen."

Her own heart ached for him, and she found it wasn't so scary to give him something in return. "Both of my parents passed away when I was in my early twenties."

"I'm sorry." The hand on her nape squeezed.

She'd forgotten it was there at all, and that probably should have concerned her. Instead, she found herself enjoying the warmth as she scooped up some pasta and sauce and offered it to him. "Want to try?"

His lips parted and she slipped the tines inside his mouth, his low rumbling growl of approval making her nipples harden.

And she found herself giving just a little bit more.

"My parents were like them."

"Like Robbie and Vivian?"

She nodded.

He didn't ask her for more details, just squeezed that hand again and smiled down gently at her. "It sounds like you were lucky to have two incredible people in your life."

Her heart stilled, lungs freezing, throat tightening for one long moment.

Then her body began working again.

"Yes," she murmured, seeing the truth in his words, understanding them as truth for perhaps the first time in her life. "Yes, Kevin. You're right. I was so lucky to have them, even if just for a little while."

"My dad was the same," he said. "Gone to soon, but amazing while he was there."

She set her fork down, placed her palm on his shoulder lightly.

"It seems like we were both lucky."

One half of his mouth turned up. "Yes."

She took another bite, chewed, and swallowed, then deliberately turned their conversation to something much lighter. "So, Hayes, now is the time for the most important question of our date. The make or break moment, as you will. Or maybe, more your speed"—she winked—"the clutch goal in overtime moment."

He tilted his head, eyes dancing. "Tell me, wise one. What is this critical question?"

"*Die Hard*," she said. "Is it a Christmas movie?"

His laughter was warm and boisterous, and Rebecca found that somehow that lovely, heartfelt laughter had managed to fill up a hole she'd never even realized was empty.

And when his answer was "Hell, yes, it's a Christmas movie," she found that the hole had overflowed, that the warmth was at risk of seeping into other holes and cracks.

Dangerous man.

Lovely man.

Generous man.

Especially when he pushed the tiramisu in her direction, along with a fork, and refused to accept a single bite until she'd had her fill.

Coffee and chocolate.

How could she resist?

How could she possibly hope to resist Kevin?

Yet, she knew she had to.

But maybe . . . maybe for that one night, she could pretend she didn't have to.

She picked up the fork and tucked every feeling, every laugh and smile close, secured them safely into that steel chest in her heart. Then she ate the tiramisu.

Every single bite.

EIGHT

KEVIN

H e held the door for Rebecca, biting back a smile when she rubbed her stomach with a groan.

"You delivered," she said. "You definitely delivered with that tiramisu."

"Well, Robbie delivered. But I know what you mean." He slipped his arm through hers, took advantage of her food coma to tug her a little closer. "However, I will take full credit for having found the place."

"As you should."

The evening air was brisk, cutting through the thin fabric of his slacks and making Rebecca shiver. Which was a convenient excuse for him to sidle closer. His mother had ingrained in him to be a gentleman, so the least he could do was his level best to keep this woman warm.

Plus, it had the added benefit of pressing all those luscious curves of hers against his side.

Fucking glorious.

Unfortunately, they arrived at his car and he had to release her to open the door. She wavered on her heels as she began to sit, three glasses of wine apparently making navigating those four inches much more precarious.

He reached over her, buckled her seat belt, cock twitching when her breath caught. If he turned his head slightly, the barest shift of his neck, he could taste that luscious mouth.

But it was too soon.

Kevin was playing the long game, and the last thing he needed to do was to make a move too quickly and—

A dart of wet heat against his throat.

He jumped, nearly clocked his head against the roof of his car.

"Mmm," she murmured, nuzzling close. "Why do you always smell so damned good?"

The twitch in his pants was rapidly becoming a problem.

He pulled back slightly, met her eyes. She had the sexiest curve to her mouth, the slightest hint of pink on her cheeks, and mischievousness in her gaze. So fucking sexy. That mouth, those eyes, that sinful body. But he could also see something else in her expression, had confirmed it when she'd wavered on her heels, long game or not.

She was buzzed.

Which was the reason he didn't close the distance between their lips, didn't give in to the bone-deep urge to taste her.

Instead, he cupped her cheek, pressed a kiss to her forehead, and backed out of the car. He closed the door, not missing the confused expression on her face as he rounded the hood and got into his own seat.

Silence as he buckled in, as he started up the car, when he handed her the cord so she could plug in her phone.

He chuckled when she lifted a brow. "I did promise you playlist privileges."

She studied him for a long moment before plugging the cord into her cell and staring down at the screen. But she didn't protest and within a few moments, the soft strains of some boy band ballad began playing through the speakers.

Kevin hid a wince but didn't protest.

He'd promised, and he always kept his promises.

"I don't get you," she murmured, barely audible.

After waiting a few moments for further explanation and not getting one, he asked. "What don't you get?"

She just shook her head in response and though he wanted to press for an explanation, though he didn't understand where exactly her mind was at, Kevin swallowed the additional questions flowing through his mind. He'd promised patience and time and on her own terms.

Guarantees he'd keep.

Even if he was damned confused as to the state of her mind.

They hadn't gotten off to a great start, he knew that. But they'd settled in and the food, the restaurant, her relaxing enough to chat with Vivian and Robbie, then banter with him . . . *that* had been fantastic. And their chemistry, or at least *his* attraction to her, was off the charts. But she'd been so reserved with him, careful to keep her distance, even when he encroached in her space that he'd been beginning to wonder if she was attracted to him at all.

Then the nuzzling.

So at the very least, she liked the way he smelled.

That was something.

He pulled out of the stall, turned out onto the road. In the opposite direction of the rink because if she was too inebriated to navigate her heels, he sure as fuck wouldn't let her drive. Luckily, he knew which neighborhood she lived in, so he had a couple of minutes before she'd realize that he wasn't taking her back to the practice facility.

Save the argument until they were close enough that it didn't make sense to go back.

Though . . . he'd be lying if he said he didn't enjoy sparring with her.

So much so that he was tempted to just drop the bomb that he was driving her home, that he wouldn't take no for an answer, dammit, and that she could just sit there and enjoy the ride.

Just picturing what her reaction might be to that level of proclamation almost had him bursting into laughter.

Almost though, because then Rebecca spoke.

And it wasn't a barb or banter or a demand to return her to the rink.

Instead, it was her address.

He braked, the car sliding to a halt at a red light, and glanced over at her. She lifted a brow. "I know the city well, Hayes. I also know I was going to Lyft from the facility to my apartment because I enjoyed the Cab Vivian picked out a little too much. If you're going to drive me, might as well not be doing it aimlessly."

"I—" Kevin shook his head. "Why do I always feel like you're a step ahead of me?"

"Ten years, bucko. Ten glorious years of experience."

"That's bullshit," he said.

The light turned green, and he started forward, eyes on the road so that he missed what was no doubt another raised brow.

"Yes, you're older than me," he said. "No, that doesn't mean you get to discount my life experience, all of the shit I've gone through, all of the growing I've done. I've been on my own since I was fourteen and my dad died."

She was quiet for a long time. "Your mom is living with you," she pointed, not unkindly. "I don't think that's on your own."

"My mom fell apart when my dad died. I picked the casket, the plot where he's buried. I claimed the life insurance, paid the bills, bought groceries." He sighed. "Even when I went away for juniors, I still came home to shovel the walk in the winter, to put out the trash cans, to mow the lawn in the summer, and to make sure the air conditioning was working."

Another extended moment of silence. "That's a lot for someone so young."

He shrugged through a right turn. "I promised my dad I'd take care of her."

"Hmm."

"Not to say I wasn't resentful," he said softly. "For a long time, I was furious that for all intents and purposes, she'd left me just as effectively as my dad had."

A beat then, "I get that."

"I think that's why she swung so far the other direction," he admitted.

Rebecca pointed. "My building is just up on the left, so anywhere here is good." Then she added, "What do you mean that she swung the other direction?"

He slid into a spot. "She pulled back. Started therapy, realized what she was doing, and then refused to let me come home. Took back the checkbook, hired a man to take care of the snow."

"She was depressed?"

Kevin nodded, regret for not having recognized exactly what his mother had been going through, not understanding that she had been more than grief-stricken. She'd needed clinical help, and he hadn't gotten it for her.

He'd kept almost every promise in his life, and certainly nearly all the important ones, but he hadn't managed to abide by the most critical one he'd made to his father.

His mother had suffered. For years. Because of him. "Yes."

"Tough."

"Yeah." He turned off the ignition. "I should have realized it sooner. Should have gotten her help."

Rebecca studied him. "Sounds like she got help on her own."

"Yup." And that had been the problem.

She'd done it on her own, no thanks to him.

"Kev—"

He popped the door, hustling around to her side of the car, and helping her out. She paused once she was on the sidewalk, pressed her palm to his chest, to the spot just above his heart.

Which skipped a beat.

"It sounds like she's good now."

A nod. "She is. Sold the house, bought her dream apartment here in the city."

Rebecca smiled. "That's great."

And yet another thing she'd done without his help, without him keeping his promise and—

"Ah," Rebecca said. "I get it now."

He frowned. "Get what?"

She shook her head. "Another time, Hayes. Just know, I'm glad she's better. For both of your sakes."

Clench.

As in *his heart* clenched.

And that damned organ was doing all sorts of leaps and lurches and rolls that evening.

"It's cold." She tugged his arm. "Walk me to my door?"

Kevin blinked. "Shit, sorry." Then he shrugged out of his coat, slung it over her shoulders, and began bustling her forward.

"Slow down, cowboy," she teased. "I may be cold, but I'm still in heels, and I work in an ice rink. I can handle a little chill."

He glared down at her but slowed. "You shouldn't be uncomfortable."

She held up a foot. "Look at these shoes. I'm *used* to being uncomfortable."

Another glare.

She smiled. "What now?"

"Those shoes might be sexy as fuck, but if they hurt, you shouldn't be wearing them." Laughter bubbled up in her chest, slipped from between her lips, and he had to admit that it might have been even sexier than those strappy little sandals.

"Oh Kevin, if you think for a second that women's fashion is the least bit comfortable, then you've confused ninety-five percent of our clothes with black leggings and slouchy sweaters."

Considering he didn't know what exactly a slouchy sweater was, he decided that the best course of action was to just nod in agreement.

And of course, she knew he was just agreeing with her.

"The truth is," she said, tugging him to a stop just inside the door to her building, "that despite their discomfort, I love my high heels. I love my lipstick. I love dressing up." Her mouth twitched. "The only difference is that I love my leggings just as much."

"I've never seen you in anything that isn't"—he paused, swapped out *fucking hot* for—"beautiful."

More laughter that drifted over his skin, slid into his gut.

"Nice try," she teased. "But I can recognize a self-censoring from five miles away."

He tugged a strand of her hair. "I've been taught by the best."

"Glad to know something stuck." She rose on tiptoe, pressed a kiss to his cheek. "Thank you for dinner." *Click* went her heels back down to the tile, and she started to turn away. "See you around—"

"Hey."

She stopped, chocolate eyes drifting up to meet his.

"You missed."

A frown tugged her brows together for a heartbeat. Then he tapped his lips, and amusement drifted across her face.

"I walked right into that one, didn't I?"

He shrugged.

The amusement left her expression. "Not sure this is a great idea, Hayes."

Kevin brushed his knuckles over her cheek. "Not sure I care."

"We work together."

"Pierre would never hold it against you."

Pierre was the Gold's owner, and also Stefan, their captain's father, and his presence alone, along with Stefan and Brit's marriage, made for the lines between work, family, and love lives getting seriously blurred.

"I'm not worried about my job," she said. "I've had job offers coming out of my ears the last few years."

He shrugged, considered the consequences of sharing the next bit of information then decided to dish anyway. "I got Pierre to write a clause in my contract when I re-signed. My position isn't at risk."

"Y-you got—" She shook her head. "In your contract?"

Another shrug. "I like to plan ahead."

"Y-you—" A pop on his chest. "You fucking idiot! How could you jeopardize something so important as your contract with something like that?"

He captured her hand when she would have smacked him again. "I know what I want, Rebecca."

She stilled.

"I knew what I wanted when I first saw you. But I knew I wasn't in a position to go after what I wanted. I knew I needed to wait." Her breath caught when he kissed her palm. "Now, I've decided that I'm done waiting."

"You—"

"I want you, baby." Unable to stop himself, he brushed his mouth across hers, but only for the briefest moment of contact. Because any longer, and he might take more and press too hard, too soon.

This was the most open she'd been with him ever.

He didn't want to fuck it up.

"I-I don't know why you'd want *me*."

"Because you're beautiful and kind and funny as shit." He rested his forehead to hers. "And because every night over the last three years, I've dreamed of you when I close my eyes."

"You—"

"So, yes. I want you, sweetheart." Just one more brush of his lips across hers. Just. One. More. "And I'm hoping that I can convince you to want me, too."

His cock was hard and aching. His mouth desperate for more.

But he pulled away, pressed the handle of her bag into her hands.

Then he pushed out of the apartment building and strode to his car, unlocking it, yanking open the door, and buckling himself in before he could convince himself to forget every notion of taking things slow and going back to finish what he'd started.

"Long game, Hayes," he reminded himself. "It's the long game."

He drove home, relieved that his mom had already gone to bed so he didn't have to come up with an explanation for why he was late or worse, why he looked like some lovestruck puppy. After brushing his teeth and hanging up his suit, he slipped beneath the comforter and turned on some boring documentary on Netflix in order to coax himself into sleep. But he couldn't help reliving the night, remembering Rebecca's smile as she'd teased him over pasta, how her tears had shattered his heart, how good she'd smelled, and how soft her lips had felt against his.

How he wanted her so damned much.

Unsurprisingly, it took him a ridiculously long time to let sleep drag him under.

And just like every other night, he dreamt of Rebecca when he finally slipped off into oblivion.

NINE

REBECCA

"You know the guys are going to give us no end of shit for this," she said.

The other Rebecca, or as the guys on the team liked to call her, Nutritionist Rebecca, sighed. "Why do I feel like a joke about how many Rebeccas it takes to screw in a lightbulb is coming?"

She grinned. "That. Except for sorting fliers?"

Nutritionist Rebecca shrugged.

"One," she told her friend. "Two is just gravy."

And avoidance. Avoiding going into the rink and potentially running into Kevin. It had been pure kismet to see her friend setting up for a community event that focused on getting kids to eat healthy and be active that morning. Seeing the other woman struggling to keep the papers in their proper spots when the SF wind was motivated to mess everything up, had given her the perfect excuse to stay outside long enough for the team to get on the ice.

Nutritionist Rebecca snorted. "I'd say you're hilarious. Except, you know I don't eat gravy."

"I know, I know. And no soy, no dairy, no meat, no—"

Fingers over PR Rebecca's lips. "Not today, Bex. Please, just don't give me shit about the diet today."

Bex froze, studied Rebecca's face. They'd done rock-paper-scissors upon first meeting and she had lost, which meant that Nutritionist had gained Rebecca privileges and she, who never *ever* let anyone shorten her name, had become Bec . . . or rather Bex since she had joked about requiring any nickname of hers to contain an "x" and Rebecca, not knowing her well, had taken her at face value. The Bec with an x had stuck, and she'd vowed to never lead with rock again. Distinguishing between them made sense, even if it had taken a long time for her to get used to it. Two Rebeccas in the same conversation were two too many, pun intended.

"I won't give you any shit. It's just—" She hesitated, not wanting to push. Rebecca wasn't normally rainbows and sunshine, but she also didn't tend to have slightly reddened eyes and an air of fragility. "Are you okay?"

"I'm fine," she said. "Just . . . can you go easy on me today?"

Bex nodded, guilt pouring through her at the inference that a request to go easy on her friend that day in particular meant she often didn't go easy on her on other days.

How many *other days* had that been true?

"Of course," she said, instead of asking her friend to validate her concerns. "Now, how can I help."

Rebecca began explaining her fliers. An elementary class was taking a field trip to the rink to learn about the team. They'd meet a few players, tour the training facility, and talk to Rebecca about the importance of nutrition.

Then they'd have some free skating time with some of the rink's training staff on hand to help with the basics. The nutrition program Rebecca had come up with was quite comprehensive for kids, but she'd also made it into a fun scavenger hunt for the third graders.

Fun with a dash of learning thrown in.

Rebecca had done good.

"The diet works," her friend muttered, stacking and unstacking the fliers again for several long moments before her shoulders dropped on a sigh. "I know it does. The guys are healthier than ever . . . despite what he says."

Another gust of wind and they both launched toward the papers, all but jumping on top of them to prevent them from flying away.

Bex waffled for a moment, trying to decide if agreeing to go easy on her friend also meant leaving that comment where it lay or if she should push for more details. Obviously, Rebecca was upset and hurt, but ultimately, Bex figured that it was better to leave it for the moment. The wind was picking up and the weather was their most prominent enemy at present.

Though she definitely *was* curious as to the *he* to whom Rebecca was referring.

"We'd better move the table inside," she said instead of pressing.

Rebecca sighed but nodded. "Yes. Clearly, this is a lesson in the futility of fighting the wind."

"Grab that end," Bex told her. "I'll help you."

They each moved, lifting either side of the length of plastic and shuffling toward the doors to the practice facility. Once they got there, the doors presented their next obstacle. Because Bex was in her usual heels and had her bag tucked under one arm, and with her coffee precariously perched on the corner, she couldn't manage to open them and hold on to the table without dropping or spilling something. Of course, the other factor was that she'd spent an inordinate amount of time that morning styling her hair—

Not because she was planning on seeing Kevin. She just liked to look good, okay?

Fine. It *definitely* was because some part of her hoped to see Kevin.

Stupid as that was.

Regardless, the shining rows of soft waves she'd perfected that morning had been effectively destroyed by the freaking wind. And now her hair was in her face and she couldn't see the door handle as she scrabbled for it with one hand, and—

The table disappeared from her other hand.

Gasping, she stopped her search for the door handle and reached for her end of the table, hoping the fliers would stay stacked, the coffee unspilled and that she hadn't just ruined all of Rebecca's hard work—

"I've got it."

Kevin.

It was as though someone had poured warm honey over Bex's head. The liquid heat slid over her scalp, dripped down her spine, soaked into her center. And yet, incongruous to the slow-moving warmth, her heart rate spiked.

She glanced up at him, getting lost in those gray eyes for a pathetically long time.

"Hi," he murmured, smiling down at her.

"Hi," she murmured back.

Fingers along her jaw. "Your hair looks nice."

Her cheeks flared hot. Rebecca Fucking Stravokraus was blushing like a child. "I thought you were on the ice," she blurted.

He shook his head. "Forwards had an off-ice session. Tape review."

"I've *got* it!"

They glanced down the table, saw the team's doctor, Gabe, was attempting to wrestle the plank of plastic from Rebecca's hand.

"Let me help you, dammit," he growled.

"You've helped me enough," she growled back.

Then they jostled the table so much in their struggle for six-feet-of-plastic-plank dominance that the fliers Rebecca had so painfully laid out were at risk of hitting the ground, along with everything else on the surface.

Bex lunged, scooping up her coffee cup.

"Shit," Kevin muttered, side-stepping so the table didn't overturn.

"Rebecca," she called loudly, knowing that it would if she didn't put an end to this. "Can you grab this door? I'll get the one inside."

Her friend froze, wide eyes drifting up and she appeared shocked that she and Gabe had an audience to their theatrics. Apparently, he was the *he* she'd been grumbling about earlier. But to Rebecca's credit, she released the table—making Gabe scramble so it didn't crash to the concrete—lifted her chin and walked over to yank open the door.

Bex didn't say anything, just silently strode past her friend and opened the other set of doors that led into the lobby.

Gabe and Kevin carried the table through, pausing to wait for Rebecca to direct them to its final location. Once it was placed to her satisfaction, Rebecca thanked them then called, "See you later, Bex," and took off back to the staff-only section of the facility.

Gabe nodded to Bex and Kevin and followed her.

"Um," Kevin began.

"I know," she said.

What the hell had that been about?

"No, not that," Kevin said. "He's been sniffing around Nutritionist Rebecca for ages."

Her brows drew together. "Then what?"

"Bex?"

She rolled her eyes. "Two Rebeccas in one conversation necessitated a nickname."

"And you just volunteered?"

She bent to fix one of Rebecca's handout piles. "No," she said.

"Then how did Bex come around?"

A sigh. "If you really must know," she grumbled. "I lost at rock-paper-scissors."

His lips twitched.

"Don't you dare laugh."

He didn't, but his smile held enough nonverbal laughter to fill the space between them.

"I need to go," she muttered, turning away to walk back to her office.

Kevin trailed her, ignoring her when she glared up at him. "Don't you have somewhere to be?"

He shrugged. "I'm doing it."

Grr.

Then, apparently, because doors had decided to become her archnemesis, she found herself struggling with the handle of the one that led to the hallway outside her office. The damn curls went into her face again, her coffee sloshed in her carafe, and her bag almost hit the floor.

"You have the most beautiful hair I've ever seen," he murmured, brushing it out of her face. "And the softest." He ran a strand of it between his thumb and forefinger. "It's like pure silk."

She shook her head, tugging the piece of hair free. "It's a mess."

"Beautiful." He snagged her bag, opened the door for her.

Rebecca didn't move, just studied his face, trying to figure this man out. He was the strangest combination of alpha and sweet, of persistent and low pressure. But the biggest thing she couldn't begin to fathom was, "Why now?"

She didn't realize that she'd spoken the question aloud until Kevin's face softened.

"Because my contract means that I'm going to be around for a while," he murmured.

That was what worried her the most. Because she *liked* Kevin, and he wasn't the type of guy a woman had a quick fling with. He was one of the good ones. He deserved care and—

A woman who could give him everything.

"You should find someone your age," she said softly.

A thumb brushed over her bottom lip. "Except, I like *you*." A beat. "And because you see me now."

He was right. She *did* see him. He'd always been hot as hell, but she'd never seen beneath the façade, and now he'd opened up to her, shared just a few things from under that surface, and it was impossible to ignore exactly how wonderful he was.

"I'm too—"

Kevin wrapped his hand around her wrist, tugged her inside the hall, and a heartbeat later she was pressed against the plaster with his body flush to hers. And there were storm clouds in his gray eyes.

"Don't you fucking dare say you're too old for me," he growled into her ear, hot breath raising gooseflesh on her nape.

"But—"

"Fuck age. Fuck playing by society's rules," he snapped. "You like me. I like you. Who gives a shit if there are a few years between us?"

"Ten," she said, hands on his chest.

She should have been pushing him away. She definitely *shouldn't* have been curling her fingers into his sweater, resisting the urge to wrap one thigh around his waist and climb him like a tree.

"I. Don't. Give. A. Fuck." He nipped her jaw, leaned heavy hips against hers. "It could be a century, and I'd still want to see where things went with you."

"You just want me because I haven't fawned over you. Because you like the chase."

More storm clouds, now with a little lightning mixed in.

"You think—" He shook his head and leaned back. "I do have a brain, and it's not ruled by my dick."

"If not that," she muttered. "Then what? I know I have a nice body. I know I'm pretty"—those were facts that she'd accepted long ago. She wasn't model gorgeous, but she took care of herself and had decent features. But that didn't mean anything other than she'd won a small hand at the genetic lottery.

"You're fucking gorgeous," he said. "But that's not why I like you. It's this"—he tapped his temple—"and this"—his heart—

"and this"—his forehead. "I breathe and I want you. I hear you laugh, and I want to find out why. I love how smart and driven you are. But more than any of those things, I can't stop thinking about you, and I can't shake the notion that you are someone I need in my life."

Her heart was pounding, her head spinning.

Aside from those being some of the most beautiful words she'd ever had someone say to her, she couldn't deny that she hadn't been able to get Kevin out of her mind.

Not since he'd made her see him.

She wanted him.

Wanted to find out what made him laugh, too, how he looked in the morning. What made him grumpy and his favorite place to vacation. And she really hoped it was a beach, because the sensation of sand sliding between her toes was the absolute best.

But aside from their age—which, based on Kevin's vehement reaction, was much less a barrier to him than she'd anticipated—there was still one other thing that she had to know.

One thing she couldn't give him, but desperately wished she could.

"Do you want kids?"

He froze, reared back. "What? No."

Rebecca's chest loosened, hope welling up inside of her. Maybe—

"Not for a few years anyway."

Her heart sank.

Hope disappeared.

And . . . there it was.

He cupped her cheek. "There's no rush, sweetheart. I just know that you're something I can't pass up. Don't we owe it to ourselves to explore—"

She couldn't even listen to the rest of his words because it hurt too fucking much.

"Come out with me again, baby. We had a good time, so let's

just keep seeing how things go. No expectations, no pressure just—"

"No."

Her throat had spikes on the inside, sharp deadly spikes that stole her voice.

Or at least made it weak.

But she'd been weak before, and she knew how to make herself strong again. Pull back, pull close, pull tight. Keep a safe distance and don't expect miracles and happy endings.

They didn't happen to women like her.

"Baby—"

"*No.*"

She shoved him, slipped to the side.

"Rebecca," he began, but she stopped him with a raised palm.

"No, Kevin," she said, spikes transforming to ice. "This isn't happening between us, and you need to accept that. Dinner once was fine. We got to know each other and nothing's there."

His palm rested on her shoulder, gripped firmly. "That's bullshit."

"Nope." She reached for her bag, but he held it out of reach.

And she snapped.

Already at the end of her rope, emotions strung tight, wanting and sadness and need knotting together with the agony of memories. Hospitals and chemo. Radiation and the news that she'd never be a mother.

Oh, she could adopt, of course, but who would let her?

The cancer would always be hanging over her.

She'd beaten the odds once, had shown clear bills of health since, but that didn't mean the disease would stay away forever. It was insidious and tricky, and it might come back. Her genetics said that much. She'd nursed her father and mother through their own fights with cancer, fights that had ultimately ended in loses.

Rebecca couldn't do that to someone else . . . and certainly not someone she might come to care for.

"Give me my bag," she gritted, eyes burning, heart pounding . . . and shattering and hurting like a motherfucker.

He lifted it higher. "Not until we talk about—"

She exploded. "*Now* who's acting their age, little boy? Give me my fucking bag, y-you *child.*"

Frost in those storm-cloud eyes, hail and snow and fucking icicles.

Kevin lowered her briefcase and slowly held it out. The moment she gripped the handle, he released it, spun away, and stormed down the hall. A burst of noise greeted her as he entered the locker room, but then all was quiet, and she was alone.

Alone.

Just exactly like she'd wanted.

TEN

"*Little boy.*"
    "*Child.*"
        Fucking perfect.

Just exactly what he'd been trying to prove to her he wasn't, and he'd all but taunted her with her bag then stomped off . . . like a child. He'd been too irritated and frustrated by her waffling moods to understand, and he'd missed the trigger that had caused her to go from warm and pliable in his arms to lashing out.

Kevin was well familiar with that particular brand of protective armor, and yet he'd missed the clues.

Of course, she'd struck at the perfect chink in his confidence.

The fact that he *was* younger than her.

He didn't give one fuck about the years between them, but obviously she did, and while he thought it was beyond stupid because they were both grown adults who could make their own fucking decisions, he also knew that she wouldn't be the last person to comment on it. And that made him fucking furious.

Who gave a shit?

But people would.

They'd comment and stick their noses into their business and—

It wouldn't fucking matter because the only thing that really did matter was what was happening with Rebecca and him. And he'd been so busy convincing himself of that fact that he'd acted like an idiot, missed the signs that she was striking out at his soft spots because he'd hit one of hers.

Inadvertently, of course.

But he'd cornered and pressed and then had been surprised when she'd struck back.

Stupid.

Fucking.

Moron.

All of his plans about taking things slow, of letting her come to him in her own time and . . . he'd blown it.

So yeah, once he'd cooled down—or rather, once he'd shot a bucket of pucks into the net, skated his fucking ass through a series of drills that were the absolute worst, then had shot another bucket of pucks at Brit. Glutton for punishment, that one, but she'd grabbed him before he'd hit the locker room and asked him to shoot at her like he had before practice had started.

And so he had.

Hadn't held back, hadn't let up. Not until that bucket was empty and they were both sweating like pigs.

Now his arms were like Jell-O, and his captain had forced him to go to a woman he liked but sure as shit didn't want to see. Mandy had taken one glance at him, straight out of the shower but still dripping sweat and had ordered him up onto a table.

"Face down. Shirt off," she muttered.

"Things I live to hear."

"Hilarious. But I've heard it all before. Now lay down and I'll rub you down—"

He snorted. "You can't say things like that."

Her fingers dug into his shoulder, just on the wrong side of too hard, and he bit back a groan. "I can say whatever I want."

The strong ass massage hurt like hell, but it made the muscles in his back relax. "Especially when without me, you'd hardly be able to move tomorrow. What the hell were you thinking, Hayes?"

"I was thinking, I either shoot some fucking pucks or I might check one of my own teammates, and nobody needs that shit."

A pause. "Is something wrong in the locker room?"

"Nothing wrong with the team," he muttered.

"Ah." She placed some sort of lotion concoction on his back, rubbed it vigorously into his skin, then followed it with a hot towel. "It's a woman."

Her words made him stiffen . . . then promptly realize it was the exact wrong reaction. He'd all but confirmed her statement.

Fuck.

"I won't press," Mandy said after a moment, and he snorted at the irony in those words. Ironic, not because she wouldn't abide by them, but ironic because the same exact sentiment had gotten him exactly nowhere with Rebecca.

"Thanks," he muttered.

"But I am here if you need to talk." She swapped the towels, went back to massaging.

"Gossip, you mean," he said.

"Gossip," she agreed. "But only because I'm so blissfully happy that I want everyone I care about as happy as me."

"You and Blane are lucky to have each other."

"True." She patted his back, telling him nonverbally that she was done with her treatment. "Cool pool. Hot pool," she said. "Then roller and out. And yes, Blane and I are happy, but that doesn't mean you can't be, too."

He shrugged into his shirt. "It does if the person I want isn't interested."

Lies.

And she knew it.

"Bullshit."

"Fine," he grumbled. "I know she's interested."

"Then what's the problem?"

He crossed the room, scooped up a towel. "She's running scared."

"Well, hun, if I know nothing else about you, it's that you've never backed down in the face of adversity."

"I—"

He hadn't really needed to overcome adversity, not like a lot of the guys on the team. His life hadn't been fraught with challenges. He'd had loving parents, a supportive group of friends, good coaches. Yes, he'd worked hard, but his path to his dream job had been relatively easy.

Mandy closed a drawer with more emphasis than was strictly necessary, the sharp *crack* making him straighten. Before he could comment, she stomped over to him and poked him in the chest. "First," she said. "I've told you guys that this is *not* the cabinet for pool towels." She took one step to the right, opened *that* cabinet —which in fairness to her snappy tone *was* labeled "Pool Towels" —pulled one out then shoved it in his chest. "Second, don't start pulling that Humble Kevin Act. You earned your spot on the team and you overcame obstacles to get here. Own that. Accept that." Her tone softened. "I know how hard it is to lose a dad, even if in my case, mine wasn't a very nice person. A lovely one, who genuinely cared about you? That couldn't have been easy, Kev."

"It—"

What could he say?

"It was what it was."

Mandy lifted a brow. "Really?"

"What?"

"It was what it was? *That's* what you're going with?"

"Well, it wasn't like I had any choice in the matter."

She sighed, punched him lightly on the shoulder. "Except you did, Kev. You could have stopped, could have given up. But you took care of your mom and you worked hard, *and* you got where you are today."

He never should have told Mandy about his parents, but

they'd spent many hours together last season when he'd been recovering from a pulled groin and she'd been helping—*cough* torturing—him to get better. Plus, it wasn't like he'd been the only one sharing. She'd told him about her dad, a former player who'd had a devastating spinal injury during a game. He hadn't been a good person before, and post-injury he'd been even worse.

But his life hadn't been like that.

Yes, his dad had died, but it had been quick and a surprise and ... there had been nothing to do except to get on with it.

So he had.

"I did what I had to do."

Mandy shook her head. "Humble Kevin." She sighed. "It's a lovely trait in a world of egotistical professional athletes. Just make sure your humility doesn't mean you don't get the rest of your dream." She turned for her office. "But, Kev, this isn't the time to not fight for your life. Otherwise, you might look back on your life in twenty years and realize you missed your only shot."

He stared after her for a long moment before going into the pool room and completing her treatment orders.

But though his time in the water was finite, the exercises on the roller an easy path to follow from beginning to end, Mandy's words swirling around his mind weren't so easy to take to heart. He knew he wasn't just going to step back and accept Rebecca pushing him away, no matter how much it had stung, but he also didn't know what the hell he should be doing.

Give her space?

Storm into her office and refuse to leave?

Funny how neither of those options seemed particularly effective.

Then, just as he'd gotten out of the hot pool, Kevin heard the tell-tale *click-click* of heels across hardwood floor. He paused, wearing only a towel around his hips, a few steps from the plate glass windows.

He was close enough to watch Rebecca pass by, close enough

to see her steps slightly falter, close enough to feel the weight of her gaze on him.

She saw that *he* saw her looking, and her cheeks turned that lovely shade of pink again.

Peaches and cream.

Good enough to taste, to lick . . . to eat.

She stilled, stared at him long enough for his dick to twitch, but just when it was becoming a coverage issue, Rebecca's chin came up, her eyes deliberately turned away, and she was gone.

But that interaction had told him enough.

Rebecca might want to be detached, but she wasn't, and *that* meant he had at least one weapon in his arsenal that couldn't fail.

It also meant he wasn't giving up on her. On them.

On what might be.

ELEVEN

REBECCA

S he was an ass.

She knew that, understood that, but it still didn't mean she was going to go back and apologize. An apology would pave the path to potential forgiveness, which would lead to more talking, and *that* would certainly lead to more bodies pressing together, mouths getting closer, tongues brushing—

And then she'd be lost.

She liked Kevin, more than she should, based on one date.

Fine. The truth was that she'd known him much longer than one date. She'd had this obsession with Kevin for three years. Well, perhaps *obsession* was too strong a word, but she'd definitely kept a closer eye on him than she'd needed to, and she'd noticed him as a man, when she didn't notice any of the other players—Brit included—as anything other than chess pieces she had to direct . . . at least in the realm of her work.

Sara had been the first to slide through her shields, followed by Mike, and before she'd realized what had been happening, Rebecca had found herself integrated into a group of friends.

But she'd still never let herself just be.

Always calculating an angle, making sure the press stayed away when they wanted privacy but was there to catch the perfect shot if and when they needed one. She had staff to manage the team's social media but still crafted a good chunk of the posts, helped the players manage their individual PR needs if necessary, had personally crafted the direction of the team's public image and outreach when she'd come on board.

The team was her baby, just not one she could hold in her arms.

Because of that, she was always at work, always *had* to work—

"That is total bullshit."

Brit's sharp reprimand, a cutting remark from someone who was no doubt tough, but whose words were rarely barbed, had come into play after Rebecca had refused to sit down and enjoy a drink with them at a team event over the summer.

She'd said she needed to take pictures, and Sara had countered that she had staff for that.

To which Rebecca had said they sometimes missed things.

To which Mandy had pointed out that Rebecca was a bit of a control freak.

The truth, which she'd admitted, followed by the refrain that she couldn't stop working or something might slip and then the team might be in a bad place—

Hence, the bullshit reply.

But it had also been followed by some brutal truth that hit home and hit hard. She'd still not sat down for the drink, but not because she'd been worried about work. Instead, she'd been rocked to her core by Brit's assertion.

"Take it from someone who knows, Rebecca," she'd said. *"This isn't work. This is hiding from the world in something you love because that shit is sure safer than putting yourself out there."* A pause. *"Trust me. I've been there and it sucked. But if you can take the leap, let down your shields . . . then the world becomes a much better place."*

The world could become a better place.

Just that easily, according to Brit.

Talk about bullshit.

Except . . . she hadn't been able to shrug off the words.

And paired with Kevin deciding to be all manly and lovely and really, fucking tempting, and she was feeling less like Rebecca Fucking Stravokraus and more like a wilting lily.

Was that even a thing?

No. Probably not.

Sighing, she began shutting down her computer and gathering up her work. Her mind having drifted to the summer, and Kevin, and how much of an ass she was meant that it was unlikely she'd be able to get back to work. Might as well pack it in and finish what she needed from the comfort of her couch, in cozy pajamas, and with *Law and Order: SVU* streaming in the background.

That, especially after the emotional two days she'd had, sounded freaking fabulous.

Plus, she had a bottle of red ready and waiting to be opened on the counter.

She slipped her feet back into her heels, shouldered her bag, then stood. Now the only thing left was to sneak out of the rink. She wanted to avoid Kevin, obviously, but she also needed to bypass anyone who might see how far off her game she was, namely Brit, Mandy, and on the off-chance she was at the facility to watch her hubby, Sara.

Her door had stayed closed for the majority of the day after her run-in with the gorgeous hockey god, but that didn't mean her coast would be clear, and so she cracked the wooden panel and carefully peeked out.

Quiet.

Lights dim.

Noise minimal.

She glanced at her watch, saw it was past six. With any luck, her escape would go unnoticed. After snagging her jacket and slipping it on—well, after that and a good thirty seconds of wrestling her bag from her shoulder with her coat half on then untangling it from the jacket sleeve then shoving her arm into the freed sleeve before finally hooking her briefcase back over her shoulder—she slipped out into the hall.

No lie, she might have been breathing a little hard after her personal WWE match.

Cute.

What *wasn't* cute, was the shriek that came out of her mouth when someone appeared at her elbow without saying a word. Someone who made every nerve on her body prickle and moisture pool between her lips.

She glanced up to confirm it was who her body told her it was, not sure if she was hoping it wasn't or thrilled when she saw it was, indeed, Kevin walking next to her.

Fuck.

Because thrilled.

She couldn't stop the little thrill from skating through her body. The blip of hope that said this thing with Kevin wasn't over before it got started.

His eyes flicked to hers, his lips pressed flat, stiffness in his spine, the line of his jaw. But he didn't say anything, just reached up, brushed his knuckles over her cheek, and while she was reacting to that gesture, he took her briefcase, slipped it from her shoulder and tossed it over his.

"What—"

One glance and her question just petered out.

Especially when he lifted a brow and flicked his gaze to the doors lining either side of the hallway, doors through which she could hear people talking, people she definitely didn't want to overhear whatever conversation they were about to have.

Because the team was like a family.

A giant family that gossiped like motherfuckers.

Not in a bad way, but still very effectively, and they'd somehow managed to avoid detection that morning—mainly because Gabe and the other Rebecca had been making a bigger scene and so no one had noticed her and Kevin.

But, case in point to the breadth of the gossip train, someone had taped up a fake prescription on the wall made out to Gabe for Romance Pills.

"Mike," Kevin murmured.

She smiled. That figured. Mike Stewart had wooed a very recalcitrant Sara Jetty and they were married with a kiddo on the way, so some would say he'd done a great job.

Rebecca knew better.

He'd done a fabulous job. So much so that the other guys on the team had gone to him for all sorts of romantic tasks, from anniversaries to proposals.

"Dr. Mike," she read the signature with a chuckle. "That man."

Kevin nodded, lips twitching as they moved on down the hall. He held the door for her and walked in the direction of her car. And no, she wasn't disappointed that he wasn't taking her to his, that he wasn't cajoling her into dinner.

Absolutely not.

He paused near the trunk, waited for her to unlock and open the driver's side door.

Then he was *there*.

Between one heartbeat and the next, he was there, pinning her between the opening and the door.

"I—"

His mouth a millimeter from hers, the wide breadth of his chest flush against hers, his scent seeping into her senses, making her head spin, her breath catch, and her pussy ache.

Oh God, he was going to kiss her.

Oh fuck, she needed that so freaking much.

The lightest brush of lips, the barest flick of tongue, and then . . . nothing. He reached across her, placed her bag on the passenger's seat, and stepped back. Knuckles on her cheek again, and her knees wobbled.

His jaw clenched.

He came close again, heat in his eyes, mouth so damned tempting—

"Goodnight, baby."

His words took a long moment to penetrate and by the time it did, he was gone.

But the longing in her mind, her heart, between her thighs didn't ever really disappear. And that night, clad in her cozy pajamas, her red wine in hand, *SVU* on in the background, work in her lap, Rebecca felt just the same as every other night before.

Alone.

Only this time, it hurt a little bit more.

———

She didn't know why she was doing this to herself.

This being retrieving a box from the top shelf of her closet that she hadn't opened in years.

Ten years to be exact.

But Rebecca found that she couldn't resist anymore. Or maybe she couldn't put it off any longer. Because of Kevin. Because he'd opened some Pandora's box inside her heart and mind and . . . she was feeling something for the first time in more than a decade.

She opened the cardboard lid, tugging the flaps so that the top suddenly popped open.

Inside was her whole life.

Or, what had been her entire life before her parents died.

Photo albums. Report cards from every grade. A few glitter-covered art projects that had been much more glittery back in the day.

But art wasn't what she was in search of.

Rather, it was the envelope she'd placed there after packing up her parents' house. Her father's signature scrawl on the front, written on the front, *To My Becky*. She'd never opened it, hadn't had the courage to read what he'd felt he needed to say to her. Not when she'd lost everything.

So, like so many other things she'd stashed behind barbed wire, she'd shoved down the memories, the loss, the desire for more.

Until Kevin.

She felt rubbed raw, and worse, she felt longing. Deep, flaying longing for something different. For a future and a past.

For Kevin.

Taking a deep breath, she tore open the flap of the envelope and read. Then cried. Then read again.

And then she began to wonder. To hope. To think she might just be able to take the plunge and, for the first time in a decade, that she might not need to be alone to be safe.

That maybe she could be safe with Kevin.

———

Dear Peanut,

If you're reading this, I've joined your mother on the other side. I'm so sorry I couldn't win this battle for you, that I've left you alone. Life hasn't exactly been kind to our family, has it? You're so young and yet have been through so much. Too much.

I've thought so much about what I'd want to say in this letter, what words could possibly make any bit of difference in your circumstance. My love for you, my daughter, is infinite. And I'm so sorry that I'll have missed so much of your beautiful life. You've given me so many lovely memories, so much laughter, so many wonderful conversations, (and never enough hugs from my Becky girl), but while I hold those tightly to my heart, I know what your illness, what losing your mother and now me, will have done to you.

I've seen the light dim in your eyes, hate the pain that has changed you, and so I want to caution you to not close yourself off to the world, to let life find you and then to grab hold of it with both hands. I know this seems like cliché advice because life has already found you in many unhappy ways.

You and your mother have been my heartbeat, and because of you both, my life has been full.

I want you to find that, sweetheart.

I don't want you to be too scared and hurt to take that leap.

Be brave, baby. Don't play it safe.

A hundred thousand kisses, two hundred million hugs,

-Dad

TWELVE

KEVIN

He got to the rink early and sat in his car, waiting for Rebecca to show.

Twenty minutes later, she did, pulling to the lot in her ugly ass silver hybrid and parking in her usual spot by the door. He waited a minute, enjoying the view of that luscious ass bending over to reach for her bag in the passenger's seat, waiting to see what color it would be today.

She had three of the same bags—black, red, and blue.

For obvious reasons—because he dreamed of fire engine lips —his favorite was the red.

Kevin only had to wait another moment before he saw.

And fuck's sake. Red.

His dick twitched. Swear to God, it was just that easy with her. She breathed, he was hard. But now, instead of storing the image to use later, he shoved out of his car and crossed the parking lot.

She was muttering to herself when he approached, looking down at her nails and grumbling something about a chip. Since they and the rest of her looked absolutely flawless, he used her distraction and her under her breath grousing to his advantage. After slipping his fingers under the handle of her bag, he tugged it down her arm and tossed it over his shoulder.

Then when she spun toward him, outrage filling her expression, he shoved her coffee into her hand.

Dirty chai, extra cinnamon.

He knew because he knew her, because he'd made it his business to know everything about her that he could discover, and also because he'd been biding his time for years, and now that she'd seen him, cried in his arms, shared a meal with him, he wasn't going to let her go.

"Kevin," she snapped, and he bit back a smile.

Snapping meant she felt something.

Feeling something was good. Feeling something was fucking great.

"Give me back my bag."

He turned and headed for the arena, leaving Rebecca no choice but to follow. After a moment and a significant amount of additional grumbling, he heard the *click-click* of her heels trailing him across the lot.

"Kevin," she hissed.

He ignored her.

She got more pissed.

That was part of the plan.

He wasn't afraid of her anger. What terrified him was being dismissed as too young, too immature, too insignificant. So, provocation. Not allowing her to ignore him and to keep pushing her until the distance she kept trying to keep between them disappeared.

Then he'd deal with why she'd shut down after he'd answered her question about wanting kids.

Because he hadn't missed that either, just as he hadn't missed the longing in her expression when Mandy and Blane had brought their baby girl to meet the team, when Sara had announced she was pregnant, when Max's son came to the rink.

They were intertwined, he knew that.

But he had to push her past her fear, past that distancing armor before she would trust him enough to spill.

So he wasn't going anywhere, and he'd keep biding his time.

And it was going to work. *Fuck*. It had to work.

He held open the door to the rink, ignoring the fire in her eyes as she stalked by him and down the hall to her office. Fine by him, especially since it allowed him a glimpse of that glorious ass. Encased in a pencil skirt and paired with heels that had slinky straps wrapping around her ankles, she was fucking incredible.

"Stop looking at my ass, Hayes."

More sharp words, and it probably said something was fucked with his brain because he couldn't deny how much he liked them.

"Stop strutting that fucking beautiful thing in front of me, and I'll consider it."

Was it possible for chocolate to turn to ice?

If so, Rebecca had that shit down.

Eyes narrowed, she stomped back to him, getting close, getting *real* close, close enough that his dick got hard. Perpetual problem with this woman. But, figuring he'd pushed her far enough, he let her snatch her bag from his shoulder and didn't say anything when she flounced away.

At least, he didn't say anything until she'd reached the door to her office.

Then he said, "See you later, baby."

"No fucking—"

He turned for the locker room before she saw him smile. That, he knew instinctively, would push her past her breaking point, and he didn't want to end up with one of those sexy as shit heels chucked at his head.

"—way."

But he couldn't resist adding, "Later, sweetheart."

A door slamming closed was his only response.

He strode in to join his teammates, a wide ass grin on his face.

The first pre-season game had finally come, and because it was pre-season and just one game in L.A., Rebecca wouldn't be traveling with them.

Kevin had to admit it was probably to avoid him.

He was the only one of the major names on the team—and what a mindfuck that was, *him* being a major name—but the point was that he would be playing mostly with rookies and third and fourth liners. The guys still trying to earn their spots.

But he'd specifically asked for a few extra games, knowing it helped him hit the regular season full bore and luckily for him, Bernard was a good coach and had accommodated Kevin's request. Eighty-two games was a long ass season, especially in a high contact sport like hockey, but he knew his body, his training routine, knew it was better for him to gear up slowly rather than jump in at warp speed.

Not sure that would make sense in anyone's head but his own. Still, Bernard had okayed it so long as Mandy watched his progress.

So, he was in Los Angeles, and Rebecca was in San Francisco, and she probably thought that his plan, fine, his *pursuit* he'd continued over the last two weeks, would be on hiatus.

However, she didn't consider his wingman.

Or men.

Or rather, wing*women*.

Brit and Sara had his back.

Hence, the text he'd received just as he walked out of his room heading down to the hotel lobby to get on the bus.

You are relentless.

From a number he didn't have programmed into his phone, but he didn't need to because his gut, his brain . . . his heart knew it was from Rebecca.

I'm not the relentless one, Red.

Two minutes passed, during which time he got onto the elevator, got off the elevator, strode across the lobby to the bus, and took his spot at the back.

No longer a rookie and as a representative "old guy," he got to ride in the back.

Yup, it was like elementary school with the cool kids at the back of the bus, but since he was one of the cool kids, it was a little easier to swallow. Plus, there was always a hierarchy, even with the Gold, where there wasn't any hazing or competitiveness or huge egos. That was sports, that was men, that—

He mentally heard Brit calling bullshit on the men part and grinned then typed out another text.

Have dinner with me.

Nothing, for long enough that he'd given up on a response, had popped in his headphones and turned on his playlist (sans boy bands), before his cell vibrated.

Will you stop pestering me if I do?

Fuck, that shouldn't make him grin, but damn if it didn't.

Nope.

A beat.

How was your dirty chai?

His phone vibrated almost immediately.

Wonderful. But Brit's shit-eating grin wasn't.

And your croissant?

Nothing. Then,

Sara is equally as bad.

He bit back a chuckle.

So dinner?

Kev could almost hear her exasperated sigh, but when she didn't respond, he sent just one more text before turning his phone to airplane mode.

Enjoy your lunch. See you tomorrow, baby.

And because he'd switched his cell to airplane mode, he didn't get her response until much later.

Lunch?

Kevin. You'd better not have arranged lunch.

You are in so much fucking trouble.

Then the one that gave him hope, along with the knowledge that it was time to go to the next step of his plan.

Thank you.

That little bit of vulnerable underbelly peeking out from beneath steely armor.

Soft Rebecca.

The fucking best.

Thirteen

Rebecca

It happened while she was still trying to find the courage to leap.

The text. The constant *buzz-buzz* of her cell as social media notifications came through.

And through.

But she was focused on an important project for the team, needed to put the finishing touches on it before she could deal with whatever fire was at her doorstep.

Then her phone rang.

Her office line.

The one that *never* rang because everyone just called her cell.

Frowning, she reached for the receiver the same moment as she unlocked the screen on her mobile and began scrolling through notifications.

Her mouth couldn't form words, her mind went blank, her heart squeezed tight and shattered into a million pieces. Someone was talking frantically in her ear, but she couldn't distinguish any of the words.

The top news story on her feed read:

Gold plane has engine failure.

She dropped the receiver of her landline to her desk and clicked the article on her screen, reading it as quickly as she could and yet, only absorbing a few heartrending words.

A bird strike . . . emergency landing for the Gold . . . engine failure . . . no contact . . . story still developing . . .

Rebecca didn't think.

Couldn't process anything except for the phone ringing after she'd selected Kevin's number.

It rang and rang, but he didn't pick up.

She hung up. Called again.

More ringing. More voicemail.

Hang up. Redial.

Hang up. Redial

Hang up. Redial.

"Fuck," she whispered over and over. "*Fuck. Fuck. Fuck.*"

Hang up—

Her cell rang before she could redial.

"Hello?" she answered, eyes so blurry with tears she couldn't see who was calling.

"Baby."

She slid from the edge of her office chair to the floor.

Kevin.

"We're okay," he said.

Her breath was labored. "O-okay."

"*Baby.*" Firmer this time. "We're all okay," he said. "You're okay."

She shook her head. She was nowhere near okay. She was bleeding out, terrified beyond reason, scared of losing him and . . . scared of never having had him at all.

"You're okay," she whispered.

"I'm okay," he said again and the first notes of panic in his tone had her mind clearing, instinct having her blurt out, "Plane crash or not, I'm still not going to dinner with you."

Silence.

Then laughter caressed her ears through the airwaves. "Baby," he murmured. "I *like* you so fucking much."

Her reply of "I know," got her another laugh before she managed to whisper, "I need to go." Her cell was buzzing in her ear, a knock sounded at the door, and when she managed to find shaky feet and hang up her office line, it immediately began ringing again.

"I know, baby," he told her. "Just . . . we're all okay, all right?"

She nodded though he couldn't see.

"Bus is here to take us to a hotel," he added. "I need to get on it."

"Okay," she said, walking to her door, resting her palm on the handle when another knock sounded. "Kevin?" she asked before he hung up.

"Yeah, sweetheart?"

"I'm really glad you're okay."

A beat then, "Me too."

They hung up, she took a moment to steady herself, and then because she was Rebecca Fucking Stravokraus, she straightened her shoulders, opened her door, and got to work handling the media circus that had just surrounded the Gold.

But even as she worked, even as she juggled a million different balls, the words in her father's letter kept coming back to her.

Be brave. Take that leap.

Don't play it safe.

Maybe once, she would have taken the engine failure as a sign to stay away from Kevin, to insulate herself against the pain of knowing that she could someday lose him. But . . . he was already in.

The risk of pain was already there. Her reaction to the news story had made that quite clear.

He'd snuck past her steel armor and barbed wire and was in. Deep.

Be brave.

Take that leap.

Don't play it safe.

That tendril of hope in her heart grew, morphing, expanding into something tangible, something she was desperate for. Hope into determination into . . . courage.

Rebecca thought that perhaps she was finally ready to leap.

Or, at the very least, she might finally be ready to take Kev up on his offer of dinner.

———

She'd learned to glance down before exiting her office.

She'd learned this after stepping right into a lovely lemon tart with fresh raspberries on it several weeks before. Her heel had gone straight through the box and she'd almost broken an ankle right there in the hall. Her intern—the one she hadn't fired because he was a fuck boy but had kept around because he'd done really good work—had almost busted a rib to keep from laughing, and she'd promptly seen red, scooped up the box, then had stormed into the locker room with the smooshed box in her arms.

Then had ignored the various states of undress—and there were a lot of states of undress since she was on the team side of the room and hadn't entered the media area—to deposit the mangled tart right in Kevin's lap.

Thus acquiring him more wingmen.

An entire team's worth.

The boys and Brit had all banded together to help Kevin on his quest to drive her absolutely insane.

"Just put him out of his misery already," Brit had cajoled the last time she'd been to dinner with her friends, *"and go out with him."*

Stefan had nodded. *"He's a good guy."*

"Plus, he's hot. Those eyes. Those abs," Mandy had said on a sigh, earning her a glare from Blane, who merely told Rebecca that, *"A guy doesn't go through so much effort for someone unimportant."*

"He's brought you coffee and breakfast every day for a month, got it to you even when you weren't traveling with the team," Mike had said, ticking the items off on his fingers as he spoke. *"Plus, he's walked you to and from your car every day he was here, found out about your sweet tooth and your love for prickly little cactuses"*—of which she now had quite an extensive collection, and it had become something the team had given her no end of teasing about— *"And that's not even mentioning the new bag."*

Her heart had flopped over in her chest at the reminder of that bag.

Stormy gray, just like his eyes, and absolutely beautifully constructed.

And expensive.

Way too expensive, but she hadn't returned it, couldn't *bring* herself to return it, not when it was so freaking perfect. It was Kevin. Lovely and gorgeous and intuitive and something she didn't have but very much wanted. And so instead of excising him from her life, his gestures had sewn him in so tightly that she didn't think she would ever be able to let him go.

She'd resisted the urge to carry that bag for all of twenty-four hours.

Then she'd transferred her stuff to into it and had found . . .

Underwear.

The slinkiest, sexiest pair of lacy fire engine red underwear she had ever seen.

Underwear, she was wearing that very day.

Because Kevin was sweet and thoughtful and kind, but he also had a wicked side . . . a wicked side she was desperate to ignore and even more desperate to explore. Hence, wearing the underwear. Hence, carrying the bag. Hence, standing on the precipice of laying it all on the table, telling him all of the dark secrets inside her and letting him decide if he really wanted all of her.

Because she had the feeling that if she dove in with Kevin, it would be forever.

Forever forever.

So when she stepped outside her office and didn't see a teeny cactus or a pastry box or a bouquet of flowers or a cup of coffee, her heart sank. The team was back from the road trip just that morning, but his absence hadn't meant that his attention had waned. The gifts had kept coming, feeding the dredges of her courage, transforming them into something much grander.

She was ready.

The plane had made her see, to consider her life without him, and she knew the risk of losing him was far outweighed by the agony of having lived without ever truly having him in her life.

So it was time to leap.

But . . . no gift on her desk or outside her door. In fact, he'd been back for hours and she hadn't seen or heard from him.

So now her heart was more than sinking because if she were admitting the truth to the universe, the thought of no more Kevin, no more thoughtful gestures or quiet escorts or sweet text messages before she went to bed was unbearable.

Had the plane scare made him reconsider everything?

No. That was ridiculous. He'd called, the packages had kept showing up during the remainder of the trip. Surely if he'd changed his mind, then that would have stopped.

Rebecca looked down again, as though something might have magically appeared in front of her feet, glanced left and right, then opened the door to her office, scanning the space to see if she'd missed something on her desk. Nothing. And when she pulled out her phone, there were no texts on the screen.

Nada.

So now she had the sinking sensation that she'd worn out her welcome, ruined her chance with Kevin.

It had taken her too long to gird her loins and jump.

"So fucking stupid," she muttered, shouldering her bag and pushing back out of her office door, grasping tightly to anger because the alternative was tears and she wasn't going to allow herself to go down that route again. "Fucking dumb ass, idiotic, moron—"

"Those are a lot of adjectives for stupid."

Her heart leaped, actually leaped in her chest.

She shrugged, tried to play it cool even though her pulse was thundering, and her knees had actually gone weak with relief. Resting back against the wall and determinedly ignoring those wobbling body parts, she quipped, "Well, I'm pretty smart for an old broad."

Gray eyes went warm, all snuggly like a cozy sweater on a cold winter day. Or maybe like that sweater on a San Franciscan summer day where the fog crawled under the Golden Gate to gather between the buildings and block out the sun.

"That's the first time you've made a joke about your age," he murmured, brushing his fingers down the outside of her throat.

Her mouth turned up, relief at Kevin being there, the contact, him smiling down at her making her normally weak filter all but nonexistent. "That's because I've finally decided that I'm okay being a cougar."

"Oh?"

She bit her bottom lip. "There are some things we need to talk about, but if you're okay with everything I tell you—"

"I'll be okay with it," he interrupted.

"*After* we talk," she repeated. "Then you can decide if you want to see where things go with us—"

"I will."

Smothering a sigh, she fixed him with a glare. "After, Kevin," she said.

A hand on her cheek, cupping her jaw, and as she was reveling in the feel of his slightly roughened palm caressing her skin, she missed his mouth getting close. But then his lips were on hers, and his tongue was sliding in to tangle with hers, and . . . it felt so fucking good.

Heat flared in her center, scorching out through her lips. Pleasure burst to life, sliding slow and liquid between her thighs. She rose on tiptoe needing to be closer, to feel him flush against her, and Kevin seemed to know exactly what she was wanting because suddenly his hand was around her waist, yanking her close, the palm on her face angling her head just right before drifting back to weave into her hair. Hard to soft, his masculine spice teasing her nose, wet and hot and—

She pressed closer, leg coming up to hitch around his hip.

Which was the precise moment he began to slow the kiss, softening his lips, gentling the hand around her waist, slipping his other out from her hair. "Fucking incredible," he murmured, resting his forehead against hers. "Your mouth is so fucking sweet, baby, but this isn't exactly where I want to be when I lose control with you."

Rebecca blinked and leaned back, realized she was pressed firmly against the wall next to her office door.

This was the second time she'd found herself in such a position, and she had to say, it wasn't a bad place to be, Kevin's hard frame against hers, his hands on her body, the evidence of his desire pressing against her stomach.

He groaned. "Baby, don't look at me like that."

She blinked again, sucked in a breath that had Kevin jumping away.

"Don't do that either," he muttered.

"Do what?"

"Breathe deep enough to press those glorious tits against my chest."

"Ew." She'd never liked that word.

"Breasts?" he asked.

"Better," she murmured. "But anyway, I like them rubbing against your chest."

Another groan, and this time he flopped back against the wall next to her. "That's precisely the problem. I'm trying to convince you that I'm old enough and mature enough to be with you, not pop a boner like a teenager."

She grinned, rolled to one shoulder to face him, then said, as serious as she could manage, "I like it when you pop a boner."

He snorted.

She snorted.

Then they were both laughing.

By the time they got themselves under control, she'd seen several heads pop out of doorways, including a few from the locker room down the hall. She saw that Kevin noticed as well, but neither of them acknowledged Brit's thumbs up or Mike's amused smirk.

"Dinner?" he asked for what might have been the fiftieth time in the last month.

She shook her head, saw his face drop.

"Drinks," she said and watched those eyes get stormy, his brows draw together. "Then if you decide that you really *do* want to deal with my shit, we can order in."

"I will."

"*If* Kevin," she murmured. "If."

"I—"

She stomped her foot. "You coming back to my place or not?"

A hard look, probably ready to push her again.

But nope, not happening.

She'd decided.

Her place or they were right back where they started.

Luckily, Kev seemed to understand that she was deadly serious because he picked up her bag where it must have fallen to the floor, slung it over his shoulder, then took her hand. "Drinks," he said softly. "Then dinner."

"I—"

He reached into his pocket and pulled out a small box.

Her jaw dropped open. "I can't—"

He plunked it in her free hand. "I got it for you," he murmured. "Regardless of what happens." Kev nudged her shoulder. "Open it already."

Rebecca glanced up at him, saw the anticipation in his gaze. "You like this, don't you?"

"Like what?"

"Always having me on my back foot."

A flash of white teeth. "I like giving you things. And I'd like to see you open this one in particular, since I normally hide around the corner out of sight, so you won't launch it back at my head."

She huffed. "That was one time. And it was your lap, not your head."

"It was damned close to my head."

Only half paying attention to where he was leading her, since it was down the hall and out to the parking lot, she used the opportunity to glare at him. "First, you put it on the ground, and I stepped on it! That tart was from Maggie's. They're like gold and we had to throw it away—"

"I left another one on your desk the next day."

She ignored him and continued. "Second, you laughed when I stormed in, and I'd almost broken an ankle. I—*ack!*"

Since she hadn't been paying attention to anything other than their general direction, being abruptly lifted into the air took her by surprise. What also took her by surprise was finding her ass on the hood of a car and Kevin between her thighs a heartbeat later.

Lucky she'd worn pants that day.

Or maybe not, her vagina said. Okay, not so much her vagina as the part of her brain that had spent the last month of her life lusting after Kevin. Because a skirt would mean he could hike it up and slid her panties to the side and—

They were in a public parking lot.

Jesus, woman, she needed to get it together.

Fingers on her cheek, a thumb brushing against her bottom lip. "What just went through your mind?"

"Nothing," she said quickly.

"You sure?"

"Yes," she snapped and held up the tiny box that he'd shoved into her hand a few minutes before. "Do you want me to open this or not?"

His lips twitched, and heaven help her if he laughed—

"Open it."

"I'm not amused—"

Warm hands closed over hers. "Open it, baby."

She shut up and pulled off the lid then promptly had to look away and blink rapidly so she wouldn't launch herself into Kevin's arms and start bawling again. Once per lifetime was enough, okay?

Her eyes flicked down, and her lungs seized for a second time.

Fuck.

How had he known?

How could he possibly know?

Sitting in the white cardboard box that fit in the palm of her hand was something she'd never mentioned to another person in her life.

"H-how did you know?" she murmured.

It wasn't expensive, though she'd been admiring it for months now on Etsy. The simple wood and resin necklace was as beautiful as it had been in the pictures, and that was saying something because the photographs on the store's page had been freaking gorgeous. But more than that, and what stole her breath, was the fact that Kevin had somehow known.

"How?" she asked again, running her finger along the chain.

How could he have known she wanted it?

"I saw it on your cell's screen awhile back."

And that admission didn't make it any easier for her to breath. "And you tracked it down?"

His expression was warm. "You looked at it a lot."

She had.

Waffling because although it wasn't expensive, it reminded her of the mountains where she and her parents had vacationed the summer after she'd been declared in remission, the summer before her mother had gotten sick, three years before her father had succumbed to the same pervasive illness. The circle of resin was filled with a miniature landscape of trees and a riverbank and wasn't like anything she had in her wardrobe.

Thus the waffling.

If she bought it, would she wear it?

Or maybe, more realistically, could she bring herself to wear it at all? Would she find the courage when it reminded her so much of that glorious month in the mountains, of hiking rocky trails and dipping her feet into water so cold that it curled her toes, of campfires and gooey s'mores with marshmallow and melted chocolate dripping down her chin. She could still feel the cool air of those late nights on her skin, see the wide-open skies and more stars in that sky than she ever imagined existed.

Being so torn, she hadn't bought it.

But Kevin had.

So, blinking rapidly and swallowing hard and staring at the stained pavement until her vision was no longer watery.

"Want me to put it on you?"

It didn't go with her outfit in the least, but she nodded and when he hooked the pendant around her neck, the weight of it was so comforting that she needed another moment. He made her so damn emotional, flayed her open and made her vulnerable.

But then he cupped her cheek, tugged her close to his chest, and held her tightly.

And *that* was what made the vulnerability bearable.

Because as much as he'd pushed her over the last month, not so sneakily letting her dismiss him, he'd never pushed too hard, never dismissed her feelings or been cruel.

He just . . . hadn't let her ignore him.

Which had been beyond annoying, of course, but he'd also taught her to trust. For the first time since her parents had passed, she actually trusted someone enough to let them in, to risk being hurt if it didn't work out, and because she knew that no matter how things turned out, he'd still take care with her emotions.

Kevin had earned her trust, and that was something special.

Then whether it was because of that or because of the necklace, or perhaps it had just been due to the full month of sweet and kind and persistent, Rebecca didn't know. What she *did* know was that instead of waiting until she was back at her apartment, instead of waiting until she had a generous pour of Cab in her glass and a beer in Kev's hand, she just blurted out the truth.

"I can't have kids. And you want them. And I can't give them to you. And *I* want them. And you're young and gorgeous and wonderful and—a-and y-you deserve th-them a-and—"

Arms banding around her, lifting her, cuddling her close to a strong chest. Soft words, gentle reassurances.

And Rebecca was crying again.

And somehow, it was okay.

FOURTEEN

KEVIN

Fuck.

Fuck.

Her sobs were destroying him.

He'd crammed them into the back of his car, not anywhere he'd ever planned on sitting when he'd bought it, but a space he'd definitely put more consideration to in the future. Not that having Rebecca pressed flush against him would ever be something he'd complain about under normal circumstances, but with those heart-wrenching sobs tearing her apart and him unable to hold her and stroke her as he wanted, the tight quarters were frustrating.

Kevin could do little more than gather her tightly to his chest and ride out the tears.

"Let it out, baby," he murmured. "It's okay. Let it all out."

And she did, her broken cries pouring from her chest, vibrating against his, her pain seeping into the air around them, scalding his skin as he turned over what she'd told him.

She couldn't have kids.

Was that really all of it?

Her big secret? The reason that she'd pulled away so fiercely? Because she couldn't have a baby?

There were other ways to make a family. Adoption, surrogacy. Fuck, he could give her a house of furbabies if that was what would make her happy. All he knew was that he wanted Rebecca, wanted her in his life, wanted her to feel complete and fulfilled, and he would do whatever it took to make that happen.

As he was processing her admission, trying to sort out why she was upset—aside from the obvious because he wasn't an idiot and understood that she was grieving not being able to do something that most women could—her tears began to slow, her sobs calm, and she glanced up at him with wounded chocolate eyes.

"I'm sorry," she murmured.

He brushed back her hair, gently wiped each cheek. "Sweetheart, you don't ever have to apologize for telling me the truth or for showing emotion."

She swallowed hard. "That was a big bomb to drop and a lot more than showing emotion."

"It was *you*, and that means it was perfect."

A sniff. "Don't do that."

Kev frowned. "Do what?"

"Don't be sweet, or I might lose it again."

He attempted and failed to hold back a smile, which earned him a smack, but since that smack was followed by a tight hug from the woman who'd become his, he just snagged her hand and pressed a kiss to her palm.

She sighed, cuddled close, and relaxed against his chest.

"Was it . . . recent?"

"What?" Rebecca leaned back slightly to meet his gaze.

"Did you just find this out?"

Frozen. She went absolutely frozen, face paling, shoulders stiffening, and fuck she was going to pull away again and then he'd have to start at the beginning to regain her trust—

"No," she said. "No, it wasn't recent."

He hesitated to ask the next question, thinking that perhaps it was time to head for her apartment for that drink before he began pressing her for more details.

Her voice was sad. "I found out when I was fifteen," she said. "But I didn't fully grasp what I lost until I was older." Eyes on his. "I shoved it down and ignored it and just got on with my life . . . until I met someone I actually wished I could have a future with."

The truth was in her gaze.

Him.

Until she'd met *him*.

The weight of that admission took his breath away.

"Fifteen?" he asked, carefully resting his forehead against hers.

"Acute myeloid leukemia," she whispered, and his gut twisted itself into knots. "I was diagnosed at thirteen. Went through treatment, entered remission, and found out I was infertile at fifteen."

"God, baby," he murmured. "I'm so sorry."

"I was lucky. I'm alive."

There was something else she wasn't telling him, but before he could ask, she pulled away, opened the rear passenger's side door and got out, eyes glued to her feet. Still in those sexy as shit heels, but he wasn't focused on her gorgeous legs or fantastic ass; he was worried about the fragility in her stance.

"Baby."

When she didn't immediately look at him, he shoved himself across the small ass back seat and out the open door.

Fingers around her wrist. "Baby."

Eyes still on the ground.

"Baby."

Stubborn one that she was, Rebecca didn't budge. And so, Kevin did what he had to do. He spun her to face him and stole that pretty mouth. Instinct drove his kiss, his gut telling him that this wasn't the time for gentle and sweet, but rather the time for him to kiss her with every bit of emotion he possessed. She needed to know he wanted her desperately and that not one thing she'd just told him had changed that fact.

So, his mouth wasn't gentle and neither was his hold.

He nipped at her bottom lip, tongue sliding inside her mouth when she gasped, stroking along hers while his arms banded around her, one sliding low to cup her ass, to encourage her closer. Hips tilting, cock aching to grind against her, Kevin rotated, pressing her against the car. He knew she felt how hard he was, knew she liked it because she did that thing with her leg lifting up, wrapping around his hips and driving him to the edge of insanity.

Never going to stop.

He was never going to stop kissing this woman.

Fucking *never.*

Except, if she pushed him away. Which she did. Two palms flattening on his chest and shoving firmly.

"Baby—" he began, leaning back down, needing her mouth, needing her to know that she wasn't broken or missing something, that she was perfect and incredible and—

"Air," she gasped. "I need air."

Oh.

Come to that, he was sucking wind, too.

"Okay, sweetheart," he said, opening the passenger's side door and coaxing her to sit down. "You get your air. I'll drive." Leaning over her, he buckled her seat belt then paused, waiting until she met his eyes. "This changes absolutely nothing between us."

Her lips parted.

"*No,*" he growled. "Nothing. We see where this goes. And it's gonna go far because you're you and that's to say, you're fucking incredible, and I'm me." He pressed his lips to hers. "Which means that when I see something I want, someone who is as beautiful on the inside as the outside, a woman who's tough and fierce and brilliantly smart, I am not stupid enough to let her go."

"But—"

"No matter what." He brushed his knuckles down her cheek. "Now, breathe, baby. Get your fix of air because I'm going to kiss you again soon, and I'm not stopping for something as ridiculous as oxygen."

She rolled her eyes. "That doesn't even make sense."

"Sure doesn't." He pressed his lips to her nose, backed out of the car, and closed the door. Then he rounded the hood, got in his own seat, and buckled in, wondering if he'd said enough, if he'd done enough to show this woman how special and wonderful she was, or if she'd retreat all over again.

But some of his worry was unfounded because after he'd backed out of the parking spot, Rebecca's hand slipped across the console and she laced her fingers through his.

That was the moment Kevin knew everything would be okay.

FIFTEEN

REBECCA

Embarrassing as shit.

Twice in the last two decades she's lost her shit, and twice it'd had been with the man sitting next to her.

Ugh.

And the worst part? He was nonplussed about it. Like it was absolutely no big deal that a woman had dropped a bomb, fallen apart on him, then dropped another bomb.

Who was Kevin Hayes?

Or more important, why had he deemed *her* worthy?

Double ugh.

Why was *she* suddenly feeling so fucking mopey? *She* was Rebecca Stravokraus, PR extraordinaire, kickass social media guru, strong, funny, independent woman, and she didn't need *any* man, let alone one Kevin Hayes. Exactly. That was *exactly* right. Mmm-kay?

She stifled a sigh because all of that was true. She was tough, smart, good at her job, and didn't need a man.

But she wanted this one.

So, she was vulnerable.

Rebecca didn't like feeling vulnerable.

Kev squeezed her fingers. "The last conversation I had with my dad, the one that wasn't in the hospital was . . . intense."

She watched his face, or the side of it she could study as he navigated the crowded San Francisco roads. His jaw was clenched and when she glanced down at his free hand on the steering wheel, his knuckles stood out on his skin in sharp relief and that tension had her doing something she'd never done with a man— because she didn't do relationships, because she didn't dare put herself in a position to care or be vulnerable—but Kevin was different, and so she leaned across the console and rested her head on his shoulder.

He gave and gave and gave, and now he was giving again. He knew she was feeling vulnerable and generous, lovely man that he was, Kevin was giving her more.

"You don't have to do this," she murmured.

The car slid to a stop at a red light, and he turned his head enough to press a kiss to her hair. "Laying it all on the table, sweetheart. Let it out, see where we stand. Wasn't that the plan?"

Her breath caught, but she nodded. "Yes."

The light turned green, but he didn't shrug her off or take the hand she was holding back. Instead, he drove the last few minutes to her apartment in contemplative silence. She wanted to ask him to finish his thoughts but didn't want to push . . . or risk another breakdown in a vehicle if her new emotional side took over. So, instead of talking or asking questions, she just enjoyed resting her head on his shoulder.

When they got to her building, she directed him into her underground parking garage and had to move when he input the code to the gate. Instantly, she missed the broad expanse of him as he pulled into the lot and parked in her spot.

Her car would be staying at the practice facility again.

Because she wasn't letting Kevin leave.

Lips twitching at the creepy thought, she glanced up and her heart rolled over in her chest. He was staring down at her, emotions in those brilliant gray eyes and everything . . . just . . . stopped.

"Hi, beautiful," he murmured.

She didn't think, didn't consider her actions. For once in her life, she didn't consider risk or optics or fallout.

She acted.

Clambering over the console—damned thing kept getting in the way—she squeezed herself between him and the steering wheel.

"What—"

Not about to let him finish that sentiment, she kissed him. And fuck but it was good. Any time their lips met, the rest of the universe just fell aside. Nothing else mattered except for the two of them and—

His hands gripped her hips, somehow pulled her closer, and any thoughts of the universe, or hell, *all* thoughts whatsoever left her brain completely. Done. Gone. Because *fuck* it felt good when he stroked his tongue alongside hers, teasing it into a dance that had her seeing stars. But she could hardly concentrate on his mouth because his hands were moving and stroking, making her alternately shiver with pleasure and shift closer to get more. One of his palms was on her back, sliding up and down her spine, fingers dipping down beneath the waistband of her slacks then under her shirt and up between her shoulders. His other was alternating between her hip, tugging her closer even though they were already pressed tightly together, and her hair, tilting her head just . . . so.

And *so* was fucking great. Incredible. The best ever.

Because it was Kevin.

Eventually, they had to pull apart for pesky oxygen, and she collapsed against his chest, heart pounding, breath in desperate little gasps.

He was no better, but considering he was used to being on the ice, working his ass off for short, intense shifts and then recovering quickly, Kev was much better off than she.

"I hate you," she panted, ear to his chest, listening to his heart still pound, but his breathing slow. "And your aerobic prowess."

He'd stilled at the first part of her statement, but the second made him roar with laughter. So much laughter, in fact, that he dropped his head to her chest and lost absolute control.

She was with him, the intensity of the kiss in the hall, of the emotions in the car, and now with their make-out session leaving liquid desire to pool between her thighs, the laughter was welcome. Also, this just in, having Kevin's face pressed against her chest while he was chuckling, the hot bursts of his breath sliding through the thin silk of her blouse, the vibrations from his amusement teasing her, reminding her exactly how close he was to her breasts, the hard points of her nipples—

His head came up, stormy eyes colliding with hers.

For one second, she thought he was going to kiss her again . . . he leaned so close that she could smell the energy drink Nutritionist Rebecca gave to all the boys after practice, but just before their lips could collide, he lifted her and plunked her back onto her seat.

"Should we go up for that drink?" he asked.

She nibbled at the corner of her mouth, gaze dropping to his, loving the way it moved when he talked, desperate to taste it just one more time.

He grinned. "We're going up."

After turning to grab her bag from the back seat, he opened his door and got out. She took one deep breath, trying to remember why it was a bad idea for her to strip Kevin naked and have her way with him in the parking lot, and reached for the handle. He beat her to it, opening her door, snagging her hand, and tugging her to her feet. But he didn't step back as she found her feet and so suddenly, she was flush against his chest, all of those gorgeous, hard muscles against her and—

Well, he wasn't helping with her resolve to not jump him right there in the parking lot.

"Come on," she said, sucking in a deep breath and releasing it slowly then snagging his hand, brushing by him, or in reality, *squeezing* past him and the door. She waited a beat for him to close up the car and lock it, then tugged him toward the elevators. She punched in the code and waited for it to come down to the garage level.

Her apartment was on the top floor and had a private elevator that she shared with only a few other tenants. Tenants whom she rarely saw.

Which was a major perk right in that moment because as soon as the doors opened, Kevin tugged her inside, rasped out, "Which floor?" To which she pressed the button for her floor with a smirk, and before her finger had even moved off the button, he'd pinned her against the elevator wall and taken her mouth.

It was caveman, him pinning her against all these surfaces and kissing her senseless, but . . . in that moment? She might as well have tossed her feminist card aside, because fuck if she cared.

Plus, she had to face facts, because kissing in the elevator was a fuck-ton better than kissing in the car.

And kissing in the car had been fucking fantastic.

The doors opened on a ding and he lifted his head, leading her out into the hall.

"Why are you smirking?" he asked.

"Because your lot has corrupted me."

Now it was his turn to smirk.

She smacked him lightly. "Not *that* way," she said. "I'm corrupted on my own enough in that department. I *meant* in my use of the word fuck."

Hot eyes on her. "Oh?"

"Look," she said, tugging her purse from his shoulder so she could pull out her keys. The gray bag he'd bought her had a special pocket for them and so it only took her a few seconds, after which, he took the bag back. "I love the word fuck. It's the perfect curse word. Four letters, punchy, versatile. But you hockey players have corrupted me. I now use it as a noun, an adjective, a verb."

He snagged the keys from her hand, opened her door. "A verb?"

Oh dear.

Or maybe oh *goody*.

Because that look on his face was . . . H.O.T.

Her nipples tightened further, aching nubs that were no doubt poking through her bra and shirt. And they were far from the only body part aching. Her lips . . . her pussy. They'd been primed and waiting, and she had to face it, quite desperate, for Kevin for more than a month now. This was *years* of wanting coalescing into this moment.

"Yes," she murmured. "A verb."

Lightning in storm clouds, but this heat wouldn't burn . . . or at least it wouldn't burn to injure. It would scorch and scald and threaten to reduce to ash, yes, but Rebecca knew it would be in the best damn way.

She closed the door, locked it, then stepped close. Really close, close enough that he had to drop her bag to the floor, close enough that her breasts were against his chest and her nipples were very happy with that development. Close enough to watch his eyes darken, to smell the fruity protein drink on his breath, to see the white scars on his face—one above his brow, another crossing his bottom lip, one on his jaw.

Her mouth brushed over them. Then her tongue.

Kevin was stock still. "A verb?" he repeated, voice hoarse, every muscle in his body like granite.

"Yes, baby," she whispered. "Maybe you can show me how that works?"

For a second, nothing. No movement, no reaction. Absolutely, nothing.

Then everything. Absolutely everything.

And she wasn't disappointed in the least with Kevin's version of that particular verb.

Sixteen

Kevin

He was spinning out of control. Rebecca felt incredible, tasted incredible, and Kevin was close to losing his mind and every bit of skill he had in the bedroom. His cock was demanding he tug off those sexy as shit slacks, spread her thighs, and dive between.

With fingers and mouth and tongue. He'd make her come as quickly as possible, lift her up, pin her against the door then slide inside and—

No.

She needed more. Better. Finesse. Care. Especially after what she'd shared.

The last damned thing she needed was him rutting against her like a fucking twat who didn't know the first thing about romancing a woman.

Rebecca needed to know she was special, important, that she was *everything*.

And so, Kev forced himself to slow way down, to unclench his hands from her hair, to slip his palm down her spine, fingers dipping under her shirt to brush against her silky skin. Her thigh had wound itself around his waist again, and he actually had to clench his teeth in order to not thrust forward and grind against her.

Slow. *Slow.*

He trailed his mouth down her throat, stopping to inhale the glorious scent that was his woman, sweet and floral and spice, then nipped at her jaw.

She jumped, fingers wrapping tightly around his arms. "Kevin?"

Tongue dipping into the shell of her ear. "Yeah, baby?"

"What"—her hands clenched, her heel dug into his ass, encouraging him closer—"the fuck do you think you're doing?"

He froze. "Um."

"I'll tell you what you're *not* doing," she said. "And that is *not* showing me the meaning of fuck as a verb."

"I want to make it good for—"

He hissed out a breath when she did a little hop and he had to react quickly so he didn't drop her when her other leg laced around his waist, pressing her pussy flush around his cock. Stars flashed behind his lids, but having to cup her ass so she didn't tip backward wasn't a tough task to bear. It felt fucking incredible to have her so close, made the urge to tear off her slacks even more intense. Especially, when she slid her hands up to his scalp, gripped tightly, and ordered, "Fuck me, Kevin. Not sweet and kind. Not soft and gentle. Tonight, in this moment, I need you to make me forget my own name."

His heart thundered in his chest, his cock went impossibly harder. "You sure?"

Chocolate eyes on his, and she nodded. "Make me forget, baby."

He could do that.

Still, he hesitated one more heartbeat. "Last chance, sweetheart."

In answer, she tilted her hips and leaned up to kiss him. Then Kevin didn't worry about going slow or wringing out as much pleasure as possible from her. Instead, he focused on the moment, on getting her so hot for him that she'd forget where she worked, what had happened earlier, everything she'd revealed. Later, he was going to find out every single thing that drove her wild.

For now, he did what he'd been imagining for fucking years. He spun, pressed her to the door, holding her there with his hips to free up his hands then kissed her with every ounce of pent up desire he'd been holding on to. She met him stroke for stroke, and when he nipped her bottom lip, she nipped his. Tongue in his mouth, soft lips moving against his. It was hot and wet and there wasn't an ounce of tentativeness.

This was Rebecca and him, and they'd cut the proverbial code.

So no hesitation. No patience. Just spiraling need and rapidly moving hands. He gripped the sides of her shirt, yanked hard enough to send buttons scattering every direction.

"Kevin!" she gasped.

"I'll buy you a new one," he muttered, more focused on the sight now revealed in front of him.

Creamy skin, luscious breasts, fire engine red lace.

He reached for her bra—

"Don't tear that one," she said, one hand coming to his. "I love this bra."

He did, too. So fucking much. But if she was aware enough that she was stopping him from tearing off her clothes, then he also wasn't doing his fucking job. His woman was brilliant, passionate, and smart, but her big, juicy brain was doing them both a disservice at the moment.

"Feet, baby," he ordered.

"What?"

A shift of his hips had her heels clacking to the ground, and he spent the barest amount of time possible making sure she found her feet, before dropping to his knees, unbuttoning her pants, and yanking them down her legs.

They bunched at her ankles like handcuffs, but he didn't give a fuck.

Not when her pussy was there at nose level, not when it was in matching red lace, not when he could see that red lace was darkened with moisture.

Fuck.

"I—"

He slid his hands in between her thighs, separating them as much as her pants would allow, and pressed his mouth to her pussy. Her sweet scent alone nearly sent him over the edge, but her against his tongue was even more dangerous to his self-control. Honey with notes of tartness, she was the most delicious meal he'd had the pleasure of tasting.

And the way she reacted . . . the scream when his tongue hit just the right spot was even better.

He didn't give her slow, he didn't take his time learning everything that made her sigh and shiver and moan. Instead, he moved fast, yanking her up the cliffside, propelling her toward an orgasm with his fingers, tongue, and teeth, stroking, licking, nipping until she stiffened and cried out.

"Fuuck," she groaned. "Holy fucking shit."

Kevin slipped off one of her shoes, then one leg of her pants. "Not yet, baby," he murmured and rose to standing. "That's now."

He reached into his back pocket, pulled out his wallet and the condom from inside it. "You don't need—"

Fuck. No, he didn't.

He dropped his wallet to the floor. "I'm clean."

"I know." A beat. "You wouldn't do this if you weren't."

And fuck if that didn't hit him right in the heart. This woman, *his* woman knew he'd protect her, knew he'd never risk her, knew—

This wasn't making her forget her name.

So, he tucked the pleasure of her words away, stowed it safely to think about later, then he got back to making Rebecca forget her name. He reached behind her, flicking open the clasp of her bra, yanking it down to expose her breasts, and bending to suck one of those perfect nipples into his mouth. Not gentle. Not slow. And once again, she exploded, cries emerging from her lips, fingers curling into his biceps, pulling him closer. Kevin switched sides, cupping her breasts in both hands, working one with his tongue and the other with his thumb until she was shivering, lips parted, words of pleading pouring off her tongue.

Straightening, he lifted one of her legs back around his waist then the other after he'd unbuttoned his pants and pulled out his cock. A beat as he waited for her to meet his gaze with a raised brow because no matter how fast they were going, he wouldn't ever take something that wasn't on the table.

Her answer came in the form of her hand snaking down and positioning him at her opening.

A tilt of her hips, a tilt of his . . . and he was home.

Fucking *home*.

He stroked into her, knowing *this* was right, that nothing would ever feel as good as sliding in and out of her.

"More," a gasped-out demand that was easy to accommodate.

He moved faster, harder, his pleasure ratcheting up, and he knew that he wouldn't last much longer, but then she stiffened again, her hips bucking and a long, low cry of pleasure bursting from her lips.

And thank fuck for that, because one, two more strokes, and he was exploding, heat tearing down his spine, incinerating him, lacing his body, his heart, his future with Rebecca's.

Because he was never letting her go.

Fucking never.

SEVENTEEN

REBECCA

She came to, spine aching from being pressed against the door, shirt torn open, bra askew . . . and her pants hanging from one leg.

One foot still had a heel on, the other was bare.

And she'd just had the hottest sex of her entire life.

Kevin was flush against her, heart pounding, skin slick with sweat . . . and still hard.

"Baby?" she asked.

"Mmm?" He nuzzled her shoulder, pressed a kiss to her collarbone.

"You . . . didn't . . ." He leaned back and raised a brow. "Finish?" God, what the hell was wrong with her? She actually felt her cheeks grow warm, and she wasn't the embarrassed type. It was just . . . she gave a shit whether he'd had a good time. No. It was more than that. She *wanted* him to have had as good a time as she had.

The other brow came up. "I finished."

"Oh," she said, eyes drifting up to the ceiling. "I—I just—"

Kevin shifted, moving away from the door, and carrying her further into the apartment. "I just what, baby?"

She dropped her head to his shoulder, feeling ridiculously stupid. "Never mind."

They stopped.

And didn't move.

For an eternity.

Finally, she lifted her head to meet Kevin's eyes.

"Did I do something you didn't like?" he asked, expression deadly serious. "Fuck, sweetheart, did I hurt you?"

"God, no," she said quickly, reaching up to cup his cheek. "*No,*" she added when it seemed like he would protest. "It was fucking incredible. I—I just couldn't help but feel you're still hard and thought that maybe . . ."

His mouth tipped up. "That I'd faked it?"

A shrug. "No, not that." Or not until he'd mentioned it. "I just thought maybe . . . you hadn't gotten there yet."

He started walking again. "I got there." A beat. "Fucking best *there* of my life."

Okay, *that* made her feel good. "But you're still . . ." Pathetically, she trailed off again.

"Hard?"

She bit her lip, nodded.

"Baby," he said, mouth curving into a smile that had her thighs clenching around his waist. "I'm twenty-four."

What the hell did that have to do with anything?

He bent to nip her earlobe. "You date a younger man, baby, you get *all* the benefits."

Oh.

She hooked her ankles together, arched slightly so the hard length of him still inside of her hit . . . just . . . the . . . right . . . spot. They both groaned, her lids sliding closed because the feel of him inside her was the freaking best, and it was a moment before she could ask, "Is a short recovery time one of those benefits?"

Another shift. More groans.

"Probably the best of them," he murmured, plunking her ass onto the back of her couch, sliding out then back in, out and in.

Then he kissed her.

And showed her that a short recovery time was a really, fucking great benefit indeed.

———

"I'll see you on Friday," he murmured, kissing her cheek a little over a week later. The bus was idling outside of the rink, ready to take the team to the arena. They were taking a road trip to Vegas, Dallas, Los Angeles, and Anaheim before returning home for an extended home stand.

But Rebecca was neck-deep in a new rollout for the team's public relations outreach, and it had been her baby over the last several months.

New technology and P.E. equipment for each of the local schools in the district.

One-to-one tablets for every student from third grade up through high school, fancy phonics book sets for the kids in kindergarten through second. But the team wasn't just providing money for the initial setup of the technology, the Gold's owner, Pierre Barie, had matched the fundraising from the campaign, and that was going into a fund for the maintenance of the equipment and periodic replacement of the books. Not to mention the P.E. equipment.

The schools would have balls for days.

She smirked, and Kevin cupped her cheek. "You're thinking about my balls again, aren't you?"

Laughing, she rose on tiptoe and brushed her mouth across his. "Yes. That I am."

"I'm proud of you, sweetheart," he said, tucking her hair behind her ear. "I know how hard you've been working on this. I'm glad your big day is finally here."

She nodded, stepped back. "I couldn't have done it without the team."

"And modest, too." He bent, kissed her once more, but just when it was getting good, Stefan's voice echoed across the parking lot.

"Beep, beep!"

They broke apart, rotated to face Stefan and his wide ass smirk. "That's the bus's horn, in case you were wondering," he called. "Wheels up, Hayes!"

Kev nodded then turned back to her and brushed his knuckles down her cheek. And God, she loved when he did that. "Bye, baby. Call you tonight."

"Bye."

Another smile and then he jogged to the bus, taking a chunk of her heart with him.

They'd spent nearly every night of the last week together, and the one that they hadn't—him with the team for a quick trip up to Vancouver, her putting the finishing touches on the rollout, which she'd titled (rather brilliantly she thought), Gold Give Back —he'd Facetimed her and they'd talked until they'd both fallen asleep.

She'd given in to him, in to her own hopes and dreams, and it had been . . . easy.

Effortless.

As though they were always meant to be together and she'd been fighting her pull to him for absolutely no good reason.

Nine nights. Five at her place. Four at his bachelor pad a few streets over. And ten glorious days wrapped up in the amazingness that was Kevin. Because they'd slept together, shared meals and made love, fucked then cuddled, watched bad Netflix shows, and . . . it had been the best ten days of her life.

Sighing, she waved as the bus pulled out of the lot then she went into the building, slipping through the side door that led to her office. It felt strange to have her bag on her shoulder, since Kev always snagged it for the walk in.

Usually before he slipped some sort of thoughtful trinket into her hand to stop her protest—a pack of her favorite gum, matching earrings to go with the necklace, a reusable coffee mug that said *Bad Bitch* on the side and was an ode to her favorite song of the moment.

He knew her favorite song. Hell, he knew *all* her favorites.

She'd asked him how many more gifts he had, and his only response had been, "Enough."

So, aside from putting the finishing touches on her project, she was taking the next three days to get a stockpile of her own. Her lips twitched as she opened the door to her office and strode in, dropping her purse on her chair. In fact, she'd already started, having slipped a little something into his messenger bag just that morning.

Her phone buzzed just as she took in the sight on her desk.

"Oh, Kev," she murmured.

A cute purple tray—her favorite color, btw—was on the corner of her desk, filled with her favorites. A mug full to the brim with steaming hot coffee, a muffin perfectly centered on a floral-lined plate, and sitting next to it was a bowl of sliced fruit.

Her phone buzzed again, and she extracted it from her purse.

I was supposed to be the one with the surprise this morning.

Her lips curved, fingers flying across her cell's screen.

I like your surprise very much. Thank you.

Barely a heartbeat before her phone vibrated.

Baby, it's too much.

It was hardly anything, concert tickets for a band he'd mentioned he liked, but nothing that could compare with what he'd done for her over the last month, the last years. She hadn't realized how much life she'd been missing out on by hiding beneath her armor. Yes, she'd stayed safe, yes, she'd had friends, but she'd never told them what she'd told Kevin, never opened up the same way, and because she'd always held back a piece of herself, there had never been as deep of connection as what she had with Kev.

She loved them, loved Brit and the other Rebecca, loved Sara and Anna and Angie. But it just wasn't the same.

For some reason, the universe had granted Kevin the key to her heart and—

Fuck that.

She'd granted him the key because he'd earned it, earned her trust, had persisted and made her realize that while she couldn't give him every single thing, while she couldn't know what the future held, what she *could* do was grab hold of the present in front of her and live life like a motherfucker.

Her cell buzzed.

Baby, you okay?

She smiled.

I'm perfect. I was just having a revelation.

A beat then,

What kind of revelation?

Rebecca didn't think, just went with her gut, her heart, and typed.

The kind where I realized how much I love you.

And nothing. Silence. Absolutely no response for several long minutes. Minutes during which she realized that she should have thought, should have used her PR skills to make the first time she'd ever told a man that she loved him a grand gesture.

Or at the very least, not a blurted, unplanned text message.

She sank into her office chair, collapsed back against the leather, and tried not to bang her head against her desk.

Kevin was into her and maybe she'd moved a little fast with the verbal or text declarations, but *they'd* moved fast. They'd gone zero to a hundred, and she *knew* he was right there with her.

Her cell buzzed.

Throat tight, she reached for it and glanced at the screen.

Baby, I'm so sorry. We were boarding the plane.

Relief poured through her, but not too much because it only took her a heartbeat to realize he hadn't said it back.

He. Hadn't. Said. It. Back.

Fuck.

Buzz. Buzz.

She jumped, saw that it wasn't a text. Kevin was calling her. FaceTiming to be precise. She scrambled to answer it, almost dropped her phone as she attempted to swipe.

But then she managed, and his face appeared on the screen.

His beautiful, smiling face.

"Baby," he said.

She bit her lip. "Sorry, I didn't mean to—"

"I love you, too." A grin. "Had to tell you that while staring into those gorgeous chocolate eyes."

"Kev." Her breath caught. Then, "Say it again?"

Amusement crawled across his expression. "You want the boys to hear? To give us shit?"

Teeth nibbling into her lip again. "Um—"

But Kev wasn't listening. Because he'd spun, and she realized he must have gone to the back of the plane to call her. Rows of airplane seats appeared behind his shoulders, and she saw the team settling in for the short flight. "Guys!" he called.

"And girl!" Brit called back.

Rebecca laughed.

"My woman just told me she loves me!"

There were catcalls and whoops.

"Finally," Mike said, moving past Kevin to find his seat, but he was smiling and lightly punched Kev on the shoulder as he went.

"I hope you said it back," Stefan said.

"Damn right, I did."

Brit's smiling face popped up on the screen. "Get it, girl!"

"Get a *room*," Max teased.

"She wants me to say it again," Kev announced.

"Oh, lord," Rebecca muttered.

"I hate to end romance time," Bernard said. "But we need to take off, so tell your woman you love her and get your ass in your seat."

Kev nodded. "Sorry, coach." He shifted to let Bernard by.

"Happy for you, son."

And then it was just Kevin on the screen again. "Gotta go, baby."

"You didn't say it again."

A flash of white teeth. "I love you, sweetheart." More catcalls and whooping greeted his words. His voice dropped, almost inaudible over the noise. "And I can't wait to tell you that every day of forever."

Her heart swelled. "I love you, too."

Warm gray eyes. "Bye, baby."

They hung up, Rebecca's gaze catching on the tray on her desk, and she burst into tears, but the good kind this time.

EIGHTEEN

KEVIN

Friday night at The Mine, and the arena was hopping.

The team was off to a great start for the season, the fans were loud, and his woman was nearby, snapping pictures of the team near the bench.

She wanted a complete set of the guys in their alternate jersey for something PR related, but Kevin didn't care. He loved having her close by at any time, but knowing she was near enough to watch the game was like a drug.

He played harder, skated smarter.

Trying to impress her.

Silly, but he hadn't had a chance to see her before the game, hadn't gotten to see her to tell her in person that he loved her.

The plane had arrived late the night before, and she hadn't been at the arena because she was getting ready for the huge press release that had happened earlier that afternoon. She'd gone to one of the schools in a low-income area to help set up the equipment, to deliver the books then had led the press conference to discuss Gold Gives Back.

With two kindergartners crawling all over her, a stack of books in each of their hands, huge smiles on their faces.

But it hadn't compared to the one on her face.

She absolutely loved kids, was great with them, and couldn't have them. Fuck, the universe was cruel sometimes.

Still, Kevin wasn't going to dwell on what they couldn't have.

He was going to cherish the fuck out of what they did have—

Shit.

He dodged a huge ass player on the other team just in the nick of time, avoiding being creamed into the boards and getting a pass off to Blue. Then he forced himself to focus on the game.

Moved his feet. Skated hard to the net, sliding back door and low to give Blue options and, like the dreaded drill from a month before, one they'd been repeating at practice frequently, he was a sneaky motherfucker. This time, the defense didn't leave him uncovered, but as he skated back, the d-man followed Kevin, moving just enough out of position that Blue had a lane into the net.

Blue drove hard, ducked around a player, lined up a shot, and . . .

Kevin lurched forward, dragging the defensemen with him, and screening the goalie at the same time the puck careened toward the net . . .

And goal!

A celly—the official hockey term for a post-goal celebration—from Blue, followed by man hugs and fist bumps all around, and a smile from Rebecca that made his heart pound. But then the game went on. More skating. More goals—though ultimately, more for the Gold than their opponents. More hockey. And more smiles from his woman.

Yeah, life was good.

———

He got off the ice, dripping sweat, but the equipment manager, Richie, had his back. He took Kev's helmet and handed him a towel before he had to ask for it.

This was because the post-game team was waiting for him to answer a few questions.

They were rapid-fire as always.

A few comments about things that went well, things they could improve on. Sound bites because there wasn't time for anything else, but Rebecca was damned good at her job, she'd given them all talking points as a basis, simple topics and suggestions they could build on. Not to filter their responses so much as to give them something to say in case they froze up.

As a rookie, especially, he'd appreciated the cheat sheet.

Now that he was more comfortable, it was still nice to have them in the back of his mind in case he was distracted, for example, by things like Rebecca looking hot as hell with her camera around her neck, tight skirt and blouse on, strappy red heels, and the gray bag he'd bought her slung over one shoulder.

He finished up the interview, said bye to the guys, then crossed over to her and slipped her bag from her shoulder.

"Hi, baby," he murmured, hesitating to touch her because he was all sweaty.

She placed her hands on his chest, rose on tiptoe, and pressed a kiss to his lips. "Hi."

Kev didn't waste a moment, just got real close to her ear and whispered. "I love you."

She shuddered but leaned back with a smile. "I love you, too."

What neither of them realized was that the cameras were still running.

———

The text message was waiting on his phone when he got into the locker room.

Dinner ASAP. Call me. You'll be bringing the woman you've declared your love to on national TV.

Oh, fuck.

Yes, he'd been avoiding his mother as of late. Yes, it hadn't exactly been difficult, not when she'd been so excited about her new life in the city that she hadn't had time for him when he did call.

She'd found a knitting club, joined a reading group at the bookstore beneath her apartment. She was getting out of the city every other week, visiting a different part of the state.

In hog heaven.

Or had been.

Until he'd neglected to mention Rebecca to her.

It wasn't that he'd intentionally kept the fact that he was seeing someone seriously from her. Things hadn't been settled between him and Rebecca until just over a week ago, and he and his mom had both been gone at different intervals during that same timeframe.

He'd planned on a dinner to introduce the two important women in his life to one another. What he *hadn't* planned on was the cameraman all but outing his relationship with Rebecca on national TV.

Mick was a good guy, probably thought it was sweet, and Rebecca often dealt in the softer sides of the guy.

And when he said national TV, it wasn't like he was suddenly on TMZ and the media would be following him. Kev didn't have that kind of pull. People, the team aside, didn't really give a shit who he dated . . . or hadn't dated up until this point.

His mother, on the other hand?

Yeah, she cared.

She might be all in on the giving him space and letting him live his own life thing, but if he told a woman he loved her, then she damn well expected to meet that woman at some point.

And usually before the declaring himself on TV part.

Shit.

He wondered if Rebecca would freak. He'd finally gotten her to come out of her shell, to accept dating him, to accept loving him, would a forced meeting with his mother make her run again?

How long could he reasonably brush her off?

His phone buzzed again.

I have your schedule. I'm expecting to see you both either next Thursday or Friday.

Apparently, he wouldn't be able to brush her off for long.

———

Kevin's fear of Rebecca running off was unfounded. He'd tentatively mentioned the dates, and she'd glanced through her calendar, replying calmly, "Thursday is easier for me."

And Thursday it had become.

His mom was cooking, and this was the first time he'd be seeing her apartment.

She wouldn't let him in to see it initially, refusing to let him past the door until she'd gotten it fixed up "just right." And walking through her door Thursday night and seeing what she'd done with the place clued him in as to why.

It was a blast from his past.

The same furniture from his childhood, just less of it, and transplanted from Minnesota. It made his heart ache, the memories bloom to life. But it was in a good way, bittersweet but nice. Because even though this wasn't home, his mother had still found a way to keep his father with them.

His mom hugged him and murmured. "This okay?"

"Perfect," he said, hugging her back. "But you know you didn't have to hold on to Dad's old recliner."

She released him. "I like it."

"It's falling apart," he said. "I swear the last time I sat in it, a spring got way too cozy with my butt."

"I didn't do it for you," she said, turning to Rebecca and putting out her hand. "I'm Bernadette. Nice to meet you."

"Rebecca, and it's so nice to meet you, too." She glanced up a Kev. "Sometimes we hold on to stuff not because it's functional, but because it's important to keep those memories alive in our hearts." A beat before she said softly, "It's silly, but I have the air freshener from my parents' car. I know it can't possibly smell like anything anymore, but I swear when I hold it up to my nose, I can still smell that scent."

Kevin's heart shattered, fucking shattered in his chest.

His Rebecca, his locked-down, armor-clad woman who'd been so tough a nut to crack, had just willingly let them both in. Really, fucking deep.

Knowing his mother couldn't possibly understand the depth of what she just revealed, Kev kissed her temple and laced their fingers together. "I fucking love you," he murmured.

She leaned into his shoulder.

"Where are your parents now, dear?" his mom asked, showing them into the living room. He sat on the couch, tugged Rebecca next to him when she stiffened.

But then she blew out a breath and relaxed into him.

"They both passed of cancer when I was in my early twenties."

Kev's heart clenched. He hadn't known that particular detail, and he knew that while they were new, while he understood Rebecca more than any other woman he'd ever known in his life, he could spend the rest of his life still discovering things about her.

"Not hiding it on purpose," she murmured. "We just never circled back to that particular conversation."

He nodded because he understood that, too. She was in with them now and she'd be all in, not one foot dipped into the deep end, the other safely on the edge of the pool.

"I'm sorry, sweetheart," his mom said. "That must have been really hard."

Rebecca nodded. "It's hard to lose people who are your world."

His mom froze, swallowing hard, and Kev brushed his knuckles over her cheek. "Yes. Yes, it is."

And then his woman, his tough but sweet woman, picked up his hand, kissed the back of it, and turned the conversation on its head. "Bernadette, did you hear that Kevin got offered a contract to model?"

"What?" His mom's eyes widened. "Really?"

"Yup," Rebecca said, grinning up at him because no fucking way was he going to *model underwear*. "For a certain very well-known underwear designer. They want to put a billboard up in Times Square."

"Times Square?" His mom clapped her hands together. "Oh my God, Kevin! That's amazing."

He narrowed his eyes in Rebecca's direction. She'd better not. She'd better—

"It would be if he was going to do it," she said with a sly smirk.

Fuck's sake. She'd done it.

"What?" his mom said on a gasp. "I mean, I don't need to see my boy in his skivvies, but how in the heck can you pass up that kind of opportunity—"

"Mom."

"It might be a springboard—"

"*Mom.*"

"Who knows what other type of—"

A timer buzzed, and thank fuck for that. "Dinner time," he said, standing up and dragging them both to the dining room table. Thankfully, his mom was distracted with getting everything ready and dropped the underwear conversation.

"So much trouble," he murmured to Rebecca.

"You'll thank me for it later."

"Not likely."

"I'll owe you one if you do it."

Now *that* was something.

Rebecca smiled up at him with sparkling eyes, took one look at his expression, and nodded. "You'll do it."

He sighed because it was true.

He'd do anything she asked of him. Even underwear modeling.

"I love you," she murmured. "Plus, this is good for your career and brand outside of hockey." Kev knew that's why she was pushing it, knew that oftentimes players' careers were cut short and that these types of outside opportunities could be critical for their future security.

He'd just hoped for pretty much anything outside of underwear modeling.

He kissed her cheek and together the three of them bustled around the kitchen, carrying plates and bowls and too much food for just the three of them to the table. Then they sat down and ate and laughed and talked, and the two women in his life got along like houses on fire. So much so that he hardly got a word in edgewise.

But that was fine.

They were both having a great time, and that was what mattered.

In fact, everything was going so smoothly that when the shit hit the fan, he wasn't even in the room. He'd slipped off to the kitchen to get a head start on the dishes, keeping half an ear out for his name, when he heard the conversation lull to a halt and his mother ask,

"Do you want kids, Rebecca?"

Kev almost dropped the plate he was washing.

Fuck.

Silence.

Then, "I'd love nothing more," Rebecca said, and he set the plate down, started hustling back to the other room. "Especially with your wonderful son, but I can't."

"Oh, honey," his mom said. "I'm sorry to hear that. Are you —are you sure? You're quite young."

More silence and he'd rounded the opening in time to see Rebecca's face, the broken look in her eyes.

"Mom—"

"Unfortunately, I'm sure. I beat cancer as a teenager, but the treatments made it so I can't have kids." She stood, pushed back her chair. "Excuse me a moment."

He reached for her, but she dodged him with a shake of her head.

A moment later, she was gone, the front door closing behind her.

EPILOGUE

REBECCA

She reclined back against the wall of the apartment, taking deep breaths, wanting to keep running, to dash down to the street, pick up an Über, and get the fuck out of there. But Kevin. *Kevin.*

And Bernadette.

His mom was so wonderful, welcoming, and sweet with a wicked sense of humor. She'd had Rebecca in stitches several times throughout dinner, had included her in the conversation so readily that Rebecca felt as though they'd known each other for ages.

Charming, just like her son.

She plunked her head back against the wall.

Sometimes it hurt less when she was closed down and alone, but the rest of the time with Kevin, with being open to the world was like a fucking drug, a high she hadn't realized she'd been missing.

And Bernadette made her realize how much she missed her mom.

So even though every instinct in her body was telling her to run, to avoid the painful memories, she straightened, sucked in a deep breath, and pushed back into the apartment just in time to hear, "Are you sure, Kev? She's beautiful and seems like a lovely woman, but the fact that she's ten years older, along with the cancer, and then not being able to have kids. That's . . . that's a lot to take on."

Slice.

Fucking hell that hurt.

But she got it, wasn't offended by Bernadette's concern for her son.

All of it was the truth.

She was a risk, a big one, and she still wasn't sure she would ever be able to reciprocate all of what Kevin gave her in kind.

"Mom," he said. "I'm going to tell you this once and then never again. I love her with every bit of my being, and I love her for so many reasons, but also partly because she said the exact same thing when I told her I was interested. Wouldn't let me get close, thought I deserved more, deserved someone whole, who could give me kids and a risk-free life—"

He stopped when she went came into the room.

"But the truth is there is no risk-free life, and I'd rather have whatever time I can have with you then never have had you at all." He came over to her. "I'm not letting you go, no matter how far you run."

Rebecca cupped his face in her hands. "I'm not running any longer, baby. But sometimes I might need a moment," she said. "Because it still hurts that I can't give you everything."

"You've already given me everything, love."

A sniff made her jump and spin around.

"I'm sorry," Bernadette murmured, wiping a finger under each eye.

"I'm sorry I won't be able to make you a grandma."

"Pish," Bernadette said. "There are many ways to be a grandma. Just make my son happy"—she came over and cupped Rebecca's cheeks—"make *you* happy and I'm not worried."

Her heart pounded in her chest, her throat beyond tight, and while she couldn't manage words, she could nod.

And then Bernadette hugged her tight and she remembered exactly how good it felt to have a mother's hug.

———

Two months later

Christmas Gold-style was wild.

A team dinner at Mike's house, a potluck with way too much food and way too many pies . . . because apparently the only thing that single guys on the team could think of bringing was pies.

As in multiple pies.

So, they were up to twenty-two pies, and Nutritionist Rebecca was looking at them as though they were Satan's spawn.

She threw an arm around her friend's shoulder. "Cheat day, remember?"

"I remember, Bex," she said or rather gritted. "Don't have to like it, though."

"I'm glad you're here," Bex said and hugged her. "I—"

She broke off with a squeal as Kevin picked her up and hauled her fireman's style from the room. Brit burst out laughing, Rebecca finger waved, and Sara called, "The mistletoe is the other way."

Chuckles followed when Kev changed directions, carrying her down the hall and into Mike's office. Sure enough, she saw when he set her on her feet, mistletoe was overhead.

And he took advantage of that, kissing her senseless until she wobbled on her heels, and he had to crush her against him in order for her to find her footing.

Which was fine.

Because she rather liked being pressed against Kev's chest, listening to his pounding heart slow.

"I wanted to give you this," he murmured after a few minutes. He set her away from him and dropped a small box into her hands.

"My present for you is back at my apartment."

"This isn't for Christmas," he said, then shrugged. "Well, I guess it is, but it isn't your Christmas present exactly. It's . . ."

He kept talking, but she wasn't listening to him or not entirely, because she'd just realized what size box he'd given her. Ring-sized. A man who she loved with all her heart had just given her a ring-sized box and—

". . . should just open it."

She blinked, still processing the ring-sized box and what it might mean, what she hoped it might mean, when he opened it.

Oh.

"It's a . . . key."

"To my place," he said, smiling brightly. "We've been spending so much time at each other's places, I thought that we should exchange keys." He sucked in a breath. "Also, I'd like you to consider moving in with me. Or me you. Or—"

Her heart started pounding again.

Not a ring, but nearly as good.

"My place is rent control."

He chuckled. "Then maybe I can finagle an invite into moving into your place?"

She tapped her chin with one finger. "Maybe. Maybe not."

Laughing, he kissed her lightly. "Always making me work for it."

"You know it." She nipped his bottom lip. "Now, want to show me how that mistletoe works again?"

"Definitely." He wrapped an arm around her waist, picked up the box. "But maybe take the key out of the box first."

Rebecca lifted up the key, and her heart squeezed. A ring with a huge diamond was dangling on the end of it. "Holy—"

Kevin dropped to one knee. "Maybe we can do the wedding thing, too?"

She gasped, momentarily distracted from the shiny ring. "That was *not* your proposal."

"No, it wasn't. This is." He grinned, picked up her hand, kissed it. "Rebecca, I love you. You're beautiful on the inside and out, you're the strongest and smartest person I know, and you've made me feel like I'm living for the first time in my life." Another kiss, this time to the inside of her wrist. "Every day, every moment, every heartbeat, I fall more in love with you. So I'm asking, pleading, begging that you'll say yes when I ask you to marry me."

She nodded, fell into his arms when he stood. Tears dripped down her cheeks, and her heart was so freaking full.

How was this her life?

Kev slipped the ring from the keychain then slid it on her finger. "Kind of need the yes though, babe."

"Yes," she gasped. "That's so much fucking yes."

"*God*, I love you." Kevin grinned, pulled her close, and then he showed her the meaning of mistletoe.

Several times over.

———

NUTRITIONIST REBECCA

She'd been trying to slip by the happy couple without ruining the romantic moment Kevin had planned for Bex. But they were right by the front door and they'd see her if she moved forward.

And the guys were behind her, along with the girls.

All of whom were perfectly lovely people.

But she'd reached her limit on socializing for the day.

Thus her pinned-in position in the hall. She was desperate to be out of here, more than desperate to get back to her empty and quiet house, slip into her pajamas, and watch Hallmark movies through the night.

God, life was so much simpler in Hallmark movies.

Kevin jumped up and kissed Bex, and when it seemed as though they were fully distracted, Rebecca made her move, slipping past them on quiet feet and opening the front door.

She'd just begun to close it quietly when a hand shot out and prevented it from shutting. Rebecca didn't scream because Kev and Bex were still only feet away, but she also didn't scream because her body already knew who it was. Her traitorous body, that was.

Gabe pushed through the opening and quietly closed the door behind him.

"You're leaving," he said.

Nope. Not doing this.

Ignoring him, Rebecca turned and started for her car. She'd purposely parked it so she wouldn't be blocked in.

Girl scout, she was. Always planning ahead.

"Rebecca."

She kept walking.

She might work with Gabe, but she sure as heck wasn't on speaking terms with him. He'd dismissed her work, ignored her contribution to the team. He'd made her feel small and unimportant and—

She kept walking.

"*Rebecca.*"

Not happening. Her car was in sight, thank fuck. She beeped the locks, reached for the handle.

He caught her arm.

"Baby—"

"I am *not* your baby, and you don't get to touch me." She ripped herself free, started muttering as she reached for the handle of her car again. "You don't even like me."

He stepped close, real close. Not touching her, not pushing the boundary she'd set, and yet he still got really freaking close. Her breath caught, her chin lifted, her pulse picked up. "That. Is. Where. You're. Wrong."

She froze.

"What?"

His mouth dropped to her ear, still not touching, but near enough that she could feel his hot breath.

"I like you, Rebecca. Too fucking much."

Then he turned and strode away.

———

Thank you for reading! I hope you loved meeting Kevin and PR Rebecca! The next book in the Gold Hockey series is CHECKED **She was in love with him. The worst part? He *knew*.**

CLICK HERE TO READ CHECKED NOW>

And if you enjoyed BREAKOUT, you'll love the sexy, sweet, and close-knit Breakers Hockey crew. The first book in the series, BROKEN, is now live!

Her life was a disaster...Don't miss the hilarious Life Sucks series, starting with TRAIN WRECK. Derek Cashette was determined to salvage the train wreck of her life...and she was just as determined *not* to let him be the hero.

DOWNLOAD TRAIN WRECK FOR FREE

I so appreciate your help in spreading the word about my books, including sharing with friends! Please leave a review on your favorite book site!

You can also join my Facebook group, the Fabinators, for exclusive giveaways and sneak peeks of future books.

SIGN UP FOR ELISE FABER'S NEWSLETTER HERE: https://www.elisefaber.com/newsletter

---

Want a free bonus story? Hate missing Elise's new releases? Love contests, exclusive excerpts and giveaways?
Then signup for Elise's newsletter here!
https://www.elisefaber.com/newsletter

And join Elise's fan group, the Fabinators https://www.facebook.com/groups/fabinators for insider information, sneak peaks at new releases, and fun freebies! Hope to see you there!

Gold Hockey Series

Gold Hockey (all stand alone)
Blocked
Backhand
Boarding
Benched
Breakaway
Breakout
Checked
Coasting
Centered
Charging
Caged
Crashed
A Gold Christmas
Cycled
Caught
Cap

Gold Hockey

Did you miss any of the Gold Hockey books?
Find information about the full series here.
Or keep reading for a sneak peek into each of the books below!

Blocked
Gold Hockey Book #1
Get your copy at https://www.elisefaber.com/blocked

BRIT

The first question Brit always got when people found out she played ice hockey was *"Do you have all of your teeth?"* The second was *"Do you, you know, look at the guys in the locker room?"*

The first she could deal with easily—flash a smile of her full set of chompers, no gaps in sight. The second was more problematic. Especially since it was typically accompanied by a smug smile or a coy wink.

Of course she looked. *Everybody* looked once. Everyone snuck a glance, made a judgment that was quickly filed away and shoved deep down into the recesses of their mind.

And she meant *way* down.

Because, dammit, she was there to play hockey, not assess her teammates' six packs. If she wanted to get her man candy fix, she could just go on social media. There were shirtless guys for days filling her feed.

But that wasn't the answer the media wanted.

Who cared about locker room dynamics? Who gave a damn whether or not she, as a typical heterosexual woman, found her fellow players attractive?

Yet for some inane reason, it *did* matter to people.

Brit wasn't stupid. The press wanted a story. A scandal. They were desperate for her to fall for one of her teammates—or better yet the captain from their rival team—and have an affair that was worthy of a romantic comedy.

She'd just gotten very good at keeping her love life—as nonexistent as it was—to herself, gotten very good at not reacting in any perceptible way to the insinuations.

So when the reporter asked her the same set of questions for the thousandth time in her twenty-six years, she grinned—showing off those teeth—and commented with a sweetly innocent "Could've sworn you were going to ask me about the coed showers." She waited for the room-at-large to laugh then said, "Next question, please."

–Get your copy at https://www.elisefaber.com/blocked

Backhand
Gold Hockey Book #2
Get your copy at https://www.elisefaber.com/backhand

SARA

"Sorry I messed up your sketch," he rumbled.

She nibbled on the side of her mouth, biting back a smile. "Sorry I stole your hand for so long."

He shrugged. "My mom's an artist. I get it."

Well, there went her battle with the smile. Her lips twitched and her teeth came out of hiding. If there was one thing that Sara had, it was her smile. It had been her trademark in her competition days.

Which were long over.

Her mouth flattened out, the grin slipping away. Time to go, time to forget, to move on, to rebuild. "Thanks," she said and extended a hand.

Then winced and dropped it when her ribs cried out in protest.

"You okay?" he asked, head tilting, eyes studying her.

"Fine." And out popped her new smile. The fake one. Careful of her aching side, she shrugged into her backpack. "I've got to go." She turned, ponytail flapping through the hair to land on her opposite shoulder.

"That—" He touched her arm. "Wait. I *know* I know you."

She froze. That was the second time he'd said that, and now they were getting into dangerous territory. Recognition meant . . . no. She couldn't.

There had been a time when *everyone* had known her. Her face on Wheaties boxes, her smile promoting toothpaste and credit cards alike.

That wasn't her life any longer.

"Thanks again. Bye." She started to hurry away.

"Wait." A hand dropped on to her shoulder, thwarting her escape, and she hissed in pain.

"Sorry," he said, but he didn't release her. Instead, he shifted his grip from her aching shoulder down to her elbow and when she didn't protest, he exerted gentle pressure until Sara was facing him again. "It's just that know I *know* you."

No. This wasn't happening.

"You're Sara Jetty."

Her body went tense.

Oh God. This was *so* happening.

"It's me." He touched his chest like she didn't know he was talking about himself, and even as she was finally recognizing the color of his eyes, the familiar curve of his lips and line of his jaw, he said the worst thing ever, "Mike Stewart."

Oh *shit*.

—Get your copy at https://www.elisefaber.com/backhand

Boarding
Gold Hockey Book #3
Get your copy at https://www.elisefaber.com/boarding

MANDY

Hockey players had the *best* asses.

No pancake bottoms, these men—and *women*—could fill out a pair of jeans. She wanted to squeeze it, to nibble it, bounce a dime—

Mandy dropped her chin to her chest, losing sight of the Sorting Hat cupcakes she'd been pondering.

Blane with his yummy ass had a unique way of distracting her.

No, it wasn't even distraction, per se. He had *always* been able to get under her skin.

And that was very, very bad for her.

"Ugh," she said, tossing her phone onto her desk and standing, knowing that she wouldn't be able to sit still now.

Nope, she needed about forty laps in the pool and a good hard fu—

Run, her mind blurted, almost yelling at the mental voice of her inner devil. *A good hard run.*

Unfortunately, the cajoling tone wasn't completely drowned out. *Some sexy horizontal time with Blane would be more fun—*

But the rest of the enticing words were lost as the roar of the crowd suddenly penetrated through the layers of concrete. Her stomach twisted. Mandy could tell, even before her eyes made it to the television, that it wasn't in celebration of a goal or a good hit either.

This was fury, a collective of outrage.

She was on her feet the moment she saw the prone form lying so still face down on the ice.

Her gut twisted when she spotted the curving line of a numeral two on the back of the player's jersey.

"Not him," she said and the words were familiar, a sentiment she had whispered, had *prayed* a thousand times before. She needed the camera angle to shift, for her to be able to see more clearly *who* was hurt. "Not him."

Then Dr. Carter was on the ice and the player moved slightly, rolling away from the camera, giving a full shot of his back and the matching twos adorning his jersey.

Fuck. Not him. Not Blane.

And that was when she saw the pool of blood.

—Get your copy at https://www.elisefaber.com/boarding

Benched

Gold Hockey Book #4

Get your copy at https://www.elisefaber.com/benched

MAX

He started up the car, listening and chiming in at the right places as Brayden talked all things video game.

But his mind was unfortunately stuck on the fact that women were not to be trusted.

He snorted. Brit—the Gold's goalie and the first female in the NHL—and Mandy—the team's head trainer—would smack him around for that sentiment, so he silently amended it to: *most* women were not to be trusted.

There. Better, see?

Somehow, he didn't think they'd see.

He parked in the school's lot, walked Brayden in, and received the appropriate amount of scorn from the secretary for being thirty minutes late to school, then bent to hug Brayden.

"I'll pick you up today," he said.

Brayden smiled and hugged him tightly. Then he whispered something in his ear that hit Max harder than a two-by-four to the temple.

"If you got me a new mom, we wouldn't be late for school."

"Wh-what?" Max stammered.

"Please, Dad? Can you?"

And with that mind fuck of an ask, Brayden gave him one more squeeze and pushed through the door to the playground, calling, "Love you!" over his shoulder.

Then he was gone, and Max was standing in the office of his son's school struggling to comprehend if he had actually just heard what he'd heard.

A new mom?

Fuck his life.

—Get your copy at https://www.elisefaber.com/benched

Breakaway
Gold Hockey Book #5
Get your copy at https://www.elisefaber.com/breakaway

BLUE

"Thanks for the ride."

"Try not to go out and get a fresh bimbo to ride tonight. I hear STIs on are the rise in the city."

Blue sighed, turned back to face her. "Really?"

She shrugged, smirk teasing the edges of her mouth, drawing his focus to the lushness of her lips. "Just watching out for Max's teammate."

He rolled his eyes. "Not hardly."

"Okay, how about I'm trying to prevent you from spreading STIs to the female populace."

"I'm clean, and I'm smart," he told her. "Condoms all the way."

"Ew."

Except there was something about the way she said it that made Blue stiffen and take notice. Because . . . he stared into her eyes, watched as the pale blue darkened to royal, saw her lips part, and her suck in a breath.

Holy shit.

"You're attracted to me."

Her jaw dropped. "No fucking way," she said, too quickly, pink dancing on the edges of her cheekbones. "You're delusional."

Blue got close.

Real close.

Anna licked her lips.

And fuck it all, he kissed that luscious mouth.

—Breakaway, https://www.elisefaber.com/breakaway

ALSO BY ELISE FABER

Coasting

Centered

Charging

Caged

Crashed

A Gold Christmas

Cycled

Caught

Breakers Hockey (all stand alone)

<u>Broken</u>

<u>Boldly</u>

<u>Breathless</u>

<u>Ballsy (April 26, 2022)</u>

Love, Action, Camera (all stand alone)

Dotted Line

Action Shot

Close-Up

End Scene

Meet Cute

Love After Midnight (all stand alone)

Rum And Notes

Virgin Daiquiri

On The Rocks

Sex On The Seats

Life Sucks Series (all stand alone)

Train Wreck

Hot Mess

Dumpster Fire

Clusterf*@k

FUBAR (March 29,2022)

Roosevelt Ranch Series (all stand alone, series complete)

Disaster at Roosevelt Ranch

Heartbreak at Roosevelt Ranch

Collision at Roosevelt Ranch

Regret at Roosevelt Ranch

Desire at Roosevelt Ranch

Phoenix Series (read in order)

Phoenix Rising

Dark Phoenix

Phoenix Freed

Phoenix: Lex Tal Chronicles (rereleasing soon, stand alone, Phoenix world)

From Ashes

In Flames

To Smoke

KTS Series

Riding The Edge

Crossing The Line

Leveling The Field

Scorching The Earth

Cocky Heroes World

Tattooed Troublemaker

ABOUT THE AUTHOR

USA Today bestselling author, Elise Faber, loves chocolate, Star Wars, Harry Potter, and hockey (the order depending on the day and how well her team -- the Sharks! -- are playing). She and her husband also play as much hockey as they can squeeze into their schedules, so much so that their typical date night is spent on the ice. Elise is the mom to two exuberant boys and lives in Northern California. Connect with her in her Facebook group, the Fabinators or find more information about her books at www.elise-faber.com.

f facebook.com/elisefaberauthor

a amazon.com/author/elisefaber

BB bookbub.com/profile/elise-faber

O instagram.com/elisefaber

g goodreads.com/elisefaber

P pinterest.com/elisefaberwrite